A SEASON TO REMEMBER

Baseball story

a novel by LES KOENIG

Table of Contents

Introduction by the Author

This fictional account takes place in an imagined town of Springtown, NY in the 1980's when baseball was still our national pastime. It had not yet been supplanted by football or basketball, with the internet and cell phones yet a ways away. More importantly, it hadn't yet been tainted by the so-called Steroid Era. In the 80's, fundamentals such as bunting and other situational hitting were stressed a lot more than in the current homer-happy generation.

Liberties have been taken in the book with respect to how the baseball season was scheduled. When I was a kid, our seasons didn't begin until the end of June and ended late August. It got so hot in the summer and the dirt on the fields was as hard as concrete. When I later coached my son Scott in Little League, his season started in April when it was cold and rainy, and ended in early June. In a (my) perfect world, you would have half the season in the spring and half ending in the fall - call it writer's privilege, adding some extra drama.

I grew up in the 1960's and baseball was the center of my life. My idol, like many of my friends, was Mickey Mantle. I have his memorabilia to this day (minus the baseball cards my mom threw away) to prove it. In the absence of any sort of social media back then that would dissect a player's private life, we only knew of The Mick's on-the-field exploits, his battles to overcome serious injuries, his leadership by example, his athletic greatness. In other words, a true age of innocence.

It was a more pristine time that many of my age preach (with no argument from me), and that was due in large part to not being stuck in front of a computer all day or using any electronic paraphernalia. You woke up, had breakfast, got dressed, ran outside, and played baseball all day in all sorts of forms - hardball, softball, stickball (either simulating home plate by drawing a square box against a wall in chalk or getting more sophisticated by playing on some sort of baseball field with a pitcher, catcher, infielder, outfielder and ump to calls balls and strikes), punchball, box baseball, you name it.

This book is dedicated to those of any age who oiled their gloves for the very first time, put a baseball in the webbing to help form a better pocket, hoping the feeling would last forever, while wanting our summers never to end.

Foreword Written in Lyric Form by Dr. Scott Koenig

My old man took my hand, we walked onto the prairie land.

A sea of faces in the crowd, the noise was heavy, but it wasn't loud.

It was baseball, a free-fall, a pitfall, the green wall, the sacred hall.

The season had just begun, a chill in the air was warmed by the sun.

The men with machines were cleaning the greens

To play on this field is a little boy's dream.

It was baseball, a free-fall, a pitfall, the green wall, the sacred hall

The cool air, the long stare, I hold the leather up to my face.

It's not fair, you don't care, will we ever see another opening day?

You round third, you're being waived home

What awaits you there is still unknown.

What once was is now faded, can we please return to those glory years?

When it was just a game.

To the men in suits who wheel and deal, no emotion is shown was it ever real?

Throwing bucks around like a ball, while the hopeful minor leaguers wait for their call.

It was baseball, a free-fall, a pitfall, the green wall, the sacred hall

At the ballpark we saw legends, waived to number 7 and 24.

The Bronx Bombers, The Brooklyn Dodgers, The Amazin' Mets, The Big Red Machine

The great pastime, it was our time, the records they chased and the pennant race.

What once was is now faded, can we please return to those glory years?

When it was just a game.

Oh how we love this game. Will it ever be the same?

It's so real, so pure, it's magical and can still be the cure.

It was baseball, a free-fall, a pitfall, the green wall, the sacred hall.

Look into the field of dreams and you will clearly see.

All of the baseball men who would have played for free.

Chapter 1

One out, bases loaded, ninth inning. The Mets are behind by one run and have a golden opportunity not only to tie the game, but maybe even to win it against the Red Sox. This of course is no ordinary game. It's game 7 of the World Series, the deciding game that will crown a champion.

Here's the scenario for the Mets. Their "clean up" hitter (the batter who hits fourth in their lineup) Washburn is at the plate, with a count of one ball and two strikes. In the on deck circle is rookie Joey Harrison, who's had a storybook start to his career after being brought up from the minor leagues because of a rash of injuries to the major league team. He batted a robust .316 while being thrust right into a heated playoff race against the Cardinals and Phillies. In the previous National League Championship series against the Dodgers, Harrison hit his eighth homerun of the post-season in game 7 along with an acrobatic defensive play at shortstop in the ninth inning to win it or the Mets.

Back to game at hand. Washburn blasts the next pitch down the third base line, but it is deftly caught by the third basemen for the Red Sox. Harrison now steps to the plate with a chance to be the hero, but also carrying the fear of failure in this most important of at bats. The crowd in the sold out stadium is all on their collective feet, with millions more watching on TV. As he steadies himself in the batter's box, he knows his concentration level must be perfect. The task immediately in front of him is all that matters now. The runners take their respective leads. The pitch comes, Harrison swings, and...

"Joey, time to wake up for school!" It's the voice of Joey's mother, Jeannie. "Joey, Joey, have you been dreaming of the big game again?? I hope you won this time, honey."

Joey replied, "Mom, how do you always know I'm dreaming about baseball.?"

"Joey, it's all you ever think about. I could bet our entire life savings and be totally confident I'd be right," Jeannie said. "Now, I'm not complaining. Your love of baseball is a wonderful thing. But I've got to get to work on time, because if I don't I highly doubt my boss shares the same love of the Mets and the great Joey Harrison to let it slide. So let's get a move on and then you can daydream all you want on the school bus."

"But mom, I would have driven in the winning run if you just let me sleep a little longer!"

"Joey, you did that in yesterday's dream."

As Joey walked towards the bathroom, he turned back to her and smiled. "Yeah, but that was only game six!"

Chapter 2

Joey lived on Dorsey Street in a town called Larock, a section of Springtown in New York.

His house was a mere two blocks from the bus stop on the corner of Jay and Main. Since he was running a little late, all his friends were already at the waiting area. Eddie Howe was always the first one there. Georgie Porter and Joey were friends since they were three, having met at the sandbox ten years prior. Ronald Carson just moved to Larock two years ago from North Carolina, which all Joey knew about was he came from somewhere much farther south. Paul Dodsworth was a close friend of Joey and shared their obsession with big league baseball as much as anyone. Paul wasn't much of an athlete, but he was the smartest one in the group. Al Gustafson was the best looking one and always attracted the most girls. Ike Eichorn's real name was Kenny but no one called him that other than his parents and authority figures. Scotty Edwards' claim to fame had nothing to do with himself, but of his star running-back brother Lawrence, who Scotty was always trying to keep up with at least in his own mind. Billy Jeffries was not only Ronald's cousin but also Joey's best friend. Billy was a tall, lanky kid and who everyone hailed as a great baseball player, except himself.

Joey and Billy first met in kindergarten and had become inseparable over the years, with the exception of that one brief fight in the second grade over something neither of them could now recall.

The boys had a daily plan to get to the bus a little early to make sure they could all get seats together, especially since it was the most crowded stop on the route. Today was an especially important day since it was March 22nd and tomorrow was the first day of baseball practice in the Springtown Little League.

Little League in Springtown was unique in that it didn't run only during the spring months like most towns. Instead, it had a first half of the season during the spring, a summer break for camp and then a second half that resumed after Labor Day. The playoffs would be the last three weeks in October, culminating with the championship series of the two final teams. There were several reasons the league ran so long, first and foremost being a desire to more closely parallel the schedule of Major League Baseball and join in the excitement of a pennant race of their own. A second thought was giving a team who got off to a slow start in the first half, a chance to redeem themselves in the second half. There of course could be a scenario where the same two teams finished each half of the season at the top of the standings, and in such a case there would be a special playoff format. But that had never happened in the ten years of this "two halves" formula, which was a testimony to the overall strong competition.

"Hey, Al Gustafson, come sit over here with me," yelled one of the girls as the group boarded the bus.

"No can do, Pamela, I've got important business to discuss with my boys," Al snapped back.

As with most all thirteen year old boys, girls were as important as anything. Even during a game, a boy could be manning a position in the field and ready for the ball to come his way, but also always making sure to be mindful of how he looked to that cute one in the stands. A young man isn't just playing for mom and dad, but his social life as well, so he's got to look good too, knowing most girls don't care about how smooth he is going to his left for that tough grounder. An athlete who plays well but also looks cool has an unmistakable air of confidence and walks with a strut. It's this quality that makes a local hero and the creation of the heartthrob.

"Whatcha reading, Dodsy?" Al asked.

"I'm studying last year's statistics from our team," replied Paul Dodsworth. "Billy led us with a .515 batting average and overall as a team we hit .303, which wasn't too bad yet we still only finished with the third best overall record. I guess we'll have to really improve our pitching and defense this season."

"I hope you're not thinking of actually playing this year, Dodsworth!" Ike Eichorn cackled. "Unless you think that having you in the line up will make the other team really overconfident, haa."

"That's right, Ike," chimed in Eddie Howe. "He's planning to use reverse psychology on the rest of the league, right Dodsy?"

"Pipe down guys. Paul is an amazing stats guy and had we all done as well at our jobs as he did, we'd have won the whole damn thing," Joey shot back.

"Oh, come on Joey, we were just messing around," Ike replied.

Billy Jeffries tried to redirect the conversation back to where it started. "Hey Dodsy, let's get a rundown on everyone else now and not just what I did."

Paul then said "OK, but instead of going player by player, I'll just pass the stat sheet around."

This was no ordinary statistical piece of paper for boys their age. It had almost every kind of data you could think of, which is really what separates baseball from all the other team sports. Baseball records are far more meaningful, serving as great conversation whether you're talking at an amateur or professional level. Even though prevailing wisdom is to only try to compare players of the same generation, baseball stats of all eras are still on a lot of people's minds, regardless of when they took place - Ted Williams, last guy to bat .400, Joe DiMaggio's 56 game hitting streak, things like that.

An interesting aspect about the sport of baseball is, there isn't a whole lot of actual "teamwork" with the exception of things like turning a double play or a sacrifice bunt to move a runner up one base. Basketball has the alley oop, football the goal line stand and hockey the give and go, among the many examples in those sports. In baseball, what can the seventh hitter in a lineup do to help the hitter who bats second? Pretty much nothing. A good baseball team blends individual talents and personalities that work themselves into a cohesive unit. It's all about chemistry. It's all well and good to have superstar long ball hitters, but every team needs "role players" too.

A championship caliber squad has to have a mix of players covering all aspects of what a team needs. "Table setters" are generally the 1st and 2nd place batters who can get on base, often via a walk or a hit. These players should be adept at bunting, able to move over runners on base. "Utility players" are typically solid fielders and smart overall players who can fill in at a number of different positions either to start games or as defensive replacements. They may not be spectacular, but they also don't hurt the team wherever they play. Ideally a utility player has a great attitude on the bench and is ready to perform adequately when called upon, even in the most dramatic moments of the late innings of a game.

A winning team more often than not has both stars and guys okay with not getting consistent playing time. It's got good players and role players. And of course it also has a coaching staff with the ability to mold all the individual talents into a champion

Here are the salient stats on the sheet that Dodsworth passed around:

Name	ABs	Runs	Hits	2B	3B	HR	RBI	BB	AVG
Billy Jeffries	66	16	34	5	2	2	17	9	.515
Ike Eichorn	61	10	24	2	2	2	13	10	.393
Joey Harrison	62	11	23	2	0	0	9	9	.371
Al Gustafson	56	8	20	3	1	0	10	10	.357
Vinnie Panzini	59	10	21	4	1	1	13	3	.356
George Porter	62	10	19	2	0	1	11	5	.306
Nick Plugman	57	8	16	1	0	0	4	8	.281

Marc Davidson	44	8	12	1	1	0	4	3	.272
Scotty Edwards	60	8	16	1	0	0	5	10	.267
Ronald Carson	57	8	15	1	1	0	4	12	.263
Chris Conley	43	3	8	0	0	0	5	8	.186
Davey Filstein	44	8	8	1	1	0	3	5	.181
Donnie Bowman	39	4	6	0	0	0	2	3	.154
Eddie Howe	43	6	6	1	0	0	4	8	.140
Totals	753	118	228	24	9	6	103	106	.303

"Hey, I definitely hit higher than .356," cried out Vinnie Panzini, who had just gotten on the bus at the next stop, along with Chris Conley and Marc Davidson.

"Stats don't lie, spaghetti stomach," Ike said.

"What are you complaining about, Vinnie??" chimed in Chris. "You had me beat by one hundred seventy points!"

"And no offense C.C., but I don't look who's behind me on the stat sheet. I wanna be among the leaders."

Everyone knew he had a bad temper to begin with, but Vinnie was ready to explode as Ike continued to get on his case. Before any punches could be thrown, Billy, Joey and Scotty stepped between the two of them and prevented it from escalating.

Vinnie shot back "No one should be afraid of a little team conflict. Think about all the scuffles we read about at NFL training camps where offensive and defensive players would go at it at practice everyday. At the end of the day, they still respected each other and stayed friends. But I don't blame you for trying to stop it if you are all scared I'll put Ike out of commission for the season with my deadly right hook!"

"I'll do my talking on the field. And besides, you have to admit you ARE a little heavy around the midsection, eh Vinnie?" responded Ike.

Vinnie smiled and said, "Just more of me to love, right guys?"

Chapter 3

There were some anxious moments for Joey during his morning classes. While there weren't any tests or anything really important, he did get caught several times for not paying attention as he spent the first half of school daydreaming. Fortunately for Joey, all the teachers liked him, especially Mrs. Harris in Social Studies. Mrs. Harris knew all too well that Joey was a baseball fanatic, so on this particular day instead of coming down hard on him for not paying attention, she decided to have a little fun with it.

"What is the capital of Iowa? Anyone know? I don't see very many hands. How about you Joey Harrison?"

"Uh, what?" Joey said snapping back to reality. "Did you call my name?"

"Why yes I did, Joey. You weren't listening?"

"Honestly, I wasn't Mrs. Harris. I'm sorry."

"I'm going to have to send a note home to your parents now, but-"

"But Mrs. Harris, please don't..."

"If you let me finish, I was going to say unless you can correctly answer a question about geography. Have you been studying the parts of the country?"

"Kinda, Mrs. Harris." Joey answered nervously. "But this is a lot of pressure you're putting on me! I'll be grounded for a week if my parents get a letter home. I can't let that happen. Especially not now with baseball season starting!"

"Well, you'll just have to concentrate real hard." Mrs. Harris replied. "Are you ready, Joey?"

"Umm, OK." Joey was feverishly trying to recall the last lesson in Geography as he awaited Mrs. Harris' fateful question.

With a smile on her face, Mrs. Harris asked "Which one of the following teams does not have spring training in Florida: Phillies, Yankees, Indians or Tigers?"

Joey answered without hesitation. "The Indians of course. They train in Arizona."

"Oh, come on Mrs. Harris that isn't fair," yelled out Al Gustafson. "Joey is a walking baseball encyclopedia."

"That's correct, Al. I gave Joey a break this time since he's usually a conscientious student, but also I know baseball practice starts tomorrow, so I let him off easy. But next time, Joey, it'll be a much tougher question."

"But you don't know enough about the sport to trip up Joey the baseball genius!" bellowed Donnie Bowman from across the room.

"That may be true, Donald," retorted Mrs. Harris. "Just know that I'm married to a big time Yankee fan."

Chapter 4

Joey stopped daydreaming for the rest of the morning, and so he got by without any further incidents. He saved his wandering mind for lunch period, and the breaks between classes. Joey even had to chuckle to himself when he saw Paul Dodsworth in the lunchroom. To anyone else observing Paul, they would have been of the opinion that he was either studying for an exam, or doing his homework in advance. Joey knew better. He would have bet his entire baseball card collection that Dodsy was working on an opening day lineup and batting order.

Joey had many, many friends, and was a fairly popular kid in and out of school. But, on a certain level, he was most content hanging with Dodsy, discussing all aspects of baseball - Major League statistics, rules, game situations, the team, and Little League itself. Joey was really a rare breed. More often than not, a person (child or adult) who is very "tuned in" to things like sports statistics can't play the game well. They become proficient in stats as a means of their escaping from their physical shortcomings. Joey, however, was a solid ballplayer. Not a superstar, mind you, but definitely one in the higher echelon. By the same token, Joey was modest about his abilities, not obnoxious, and certainly not a bragger. This would greatly account for his popularity. He had a certain way about him that was admirable.

As close as Joey and Dodsy were, Joey decided to let him be for now. Anyway, there were still fifteen minutes left to the lunch period. Joey opted to walk outside to the ballfields.

There is just something about a ballfield that can "turn on" a lover of the game. Whether driving by in a car, looking out the window of an airplane, or entering a stadium, the sight of a baseball diamond can do wonders for both young and old alike. A youngster can daydream about his next game. An adult draws a direct line to his child-hood. There is a feeling of serenity, of beauty, of a majestic springtime day on a ball field.

Chapter 5

Lou Skinner had been on the phone practically all day at work, due to his secretary Helen being out sick.

"I'll no doubt win the Alexander Graham Bell award for phone usage," mused Lou to himself during one of those rare moments off the phone.

In reality, Lou knew he shouldn't complain. His job as Senior Buyer at the Larock College Bookstore ordinarily left him with considerable free time, save for the real rush times of the year (July and November), when the entire staff scrambled to make sure all the orders they'd placed were filled before the next semesters would begin.

This had been Lou's fifth year on the job, and for the last four of them, Lou was also involved as manager of the Larock Mets baseball team. The job conveniently allowed Lou to be on hand for all games, whether weeknights at 5:30PM, or on Saturdays and Sundays, plus practices. Practices ran Saturday mornings before the season started, plus two to three times a week during the season.

Lou loved baseball, and as a matter of fact, participated in a Sunday morning adult softball league. At thirty five years of age, Lou Skinner was a jock at heart, with an understanding and supportive wife in Lisa, and two children - Peter, age six, and Amy, age four. The children, even at their early stages, seemed to have a penchant for sports. As a matter of fact, Peter would be starting T-Ball this year. This is a beginners' league where the youngsters get their initial taste of organized ball by joining a team, getting shirts and hats, and playing an actual game by hitting a baseball off a rubber tee and running the bases, playing the field, and all those other sorts of baseball things.

Lou never got tired of this kind of life, which obviously was heavily devoted to baseball. It was never a chore or a drudgery to him. On the contrary, practices and games were something he was always looking forward to.

The parents all liked and respected Lou. He seemed, to them, to be forever fair to all the boys regardless of their individual skill levels. He was somewhat of a disciplinarian during practice, but he also possessed a keen sense of humor, and never let the kids (or himself) forget that when all was said and done, it was still only a game, and these were only kids. The important things were: Did the boys get anything positive out of each season? Did the average or sub-average players show improvement? Did the superior players correct any deficient area of their game, no matter how relatively insignificant? Did they all have fun? Lou enjoyed winning as much as anyone else, but these questions were never to be compromised in his mind.

Lou glanced at his watch, and happily noticed that it was just about time to go home. Tonight would be an early night at the Skinner house - a quick dinner, a "mock" wrestling match with Peter, a bedtime story to Lisa (actually, two: one read, the other made up), a scan of the daily newspaper, some television mixed in with conversation with Lisa, and then to sleep. Most importantly, there would be the ritual of waiting for the Saturday weather report. Luckily, the outlook called for clear skies with temperatures hovering in the high 50's. Every coach fears an over-abundance of bad weather before the season starts, when practices are most important, as players try to get their timing down pat.

Just then, the phone rang. Oh, no, not another call, thought Lou. Don't they know I'm winding down on a Friday? He grudgingly picked up the receiver. "Hi, honey," said the caller at the other end, unmistakably the voice of Lisa. "How's it going?"

"Hectic, babe," Lou replied. "If Helen knew how invaluable her presence was, she'd have a swelled head. The phones have been ringing off the hook since I got here this morning. This salesman trying to make an appointment, that student asking if a certain book was in."

"Sounds pretty normal to me," said Lisa.

"The type of call, yes, the amount of them, no. Or, maybe this is normal, because I don't usually answer most of them when Helen's here."

"Do you think she'll be back to work on Monday?"

"She'd better be, or I'll become a full-fledged candidate for the looney bin."

"Anyway, honey, I'm sure it made the day go by super fast. Are you leaving now?"

"In about fifteen minutes. I've got to total up the orders and straighten up. What's going on?"

"Two things. Davey Filstein's mother called. He has a dentist appointment at 9:30, so he won't be at practice tomorrow until about 10:30."

"Well," answered Lou, "Davey's one of my best fielders, and I normally begin my practices with fielding drills. He'll definitely be in time for hitting, which he's got to improve on. What's the second thing?"

"Numero dos. Can you pick up something on the way home? I've been busy all day and haven't had a chance to cook."

Lisa's being busy all day probably consisted of marathon calls to her friends, but Lou was tolerant of this stuff, since she never complained about Lou and his sports - coaching, playing, watching, or reading. In truth, Lisa was remarkable in that the Little League games, at least at this juncture in their lives, did not involve their own kids. There were not too many women around who would be so supportive and involved in such a program, under those circumstances. Lou knew it, and this was (among other reasons), why he loved her.

"What do you want, pizza, or Chinese food?"

"I would lean towards Chinese, but the kids would prefer pizza, so guess what my answer is?"

"Pizza."

"You've got it. See you when?"

"Figure around six o'clock."

"Bye, honey."

"See ya."

Chapter 6

As Lou drove home after picking up the pizza (half plain for the kids, half with the "works" for Lou and Lisa), he began reminiscing to himself about how he'd first gotten involved in managing this team. Five years ago, he'd driven past the ballfield during a regular season game. He found himself in just the right mood to stop and watch. As Lou got out of his car, he witnessed an ugly scene. The manager of one of the teams was vociferously shouting at a boy on his own squad. The kid sat on the bench, crying. It wasn't until several minutes later that Lou had learned the principals involved were father and son. Apparently, the boy had committed a costly base running error, and his father couldn't control himself, lashing out at his own son. The man's outburst stunned everyone so much, there was dead silence all around. In a split second, these thoughts flashed through Lou's mind:

1. What this man is doing to that boy is totally wrong, no matter what mistake the boy had made.

2. A father will always display much more emotion (both positive and negative) with his own child.

3. I definitely want to manage, but I'm probably better off doing it with kids other than my own, so that I can not only be instructive, but impartial and objective as well.

Lou had vacated the field almost immediately after having viewed the unfortunate incident, driven home, and proceeded to call the league right away, inquiring about managing a team the following year.

Snapping back to reality, and with the aroma of the pizza pervading his car as he veered into his driveway, Lou smiled to himself, thinking that it's been four years of great fulfillment: Exciting baseball seasons with remarkably coachable kids intertwined with a great family life. No championships yet, but always competitive squads.

Ask any person who has ever coached kids, and you'll get the same response. The best ages to coach are the 12 to 13 year olds. This age group is old enough to really be taught the finer points of the game (bunting, hitting the cutoff man, lining up the throw etc.), yet young enough so that their diversions (girls, appearance) are limited. Obviously, there is no substitute for talent (speed, power, coordination, throwing arm). But, assuming you have teams that are fairly equal in these areas, it is the team that plays with "smarts" and executes their plays that'll win most of the time. So, when Lou was thinking about his "coachable kids," he was thankful for their collective willingness to learn, their cooperation, and their overall attitude.

Lou unlocked the door to his house, and immediately heard the only other sounds that mattered to him besides "Play Ball."

"Daddy, you bring the pizza?" barked out Peter, pronouncing it as though the first syllable rhymes with liz (as in lizard).

"Yeah, daddy, I want my slice cut," chimed in Amy. Amy's appetite was limited in all aspects of food, and her intake of pizza (unless she was starving) consisted of a single slice, cut in half. Peter was good for her uneaten half plus one of his own, leaving (for all you math majors) six left. Lisa and Lou would each have three, with Lou having the easier go of it.

Shortly after dinner had ended, Lou was to be found lying on the floor in Amy's room, putting together a game for her that they'd bought last weekend. Why were instructions for a child's toy written at the level of a nuclear physicist, Lou wondered. After considerable struggling, it was assembled. With Amy now content, Lou moved into Peter's room, for one of their weekly rituals, the Friday night wrestling match. Somehow, Peter was undefeated. This one would end like all the matches that had preceded it, with Peter emerging victorious, but Lou decided to infuse some drama by winning the first of a two out of three falls contest. As Peter was putting the finishing touches on his win by leaping from his bed onto Lou's back, and turning him over for the pin, Lou thought to himself: Pretty soon, Pete will be old enough to know I'm letting him win, so I'll have to change my tactics. Unless, of course, if by that time I'm too old to stop him.

Chapter 7

Joey Harrison lay in his bed Saturday morning at 7:30. Although he could have comfortably slept at least another hour and still be at the ballfield by 9:30, he didn't. At the top of his thought list: How to improve his batting average this year over last. Even though he garnered the third highest batting average on the team, and had made the All-Star squad, Joey was disappointed in his own performance.

"I could have done better," he often told Dodsy, Lou Skinner, his parents, and, basically, anybody else who would listen. Joey was one determined son of a gun, as he gripped a baseball in his bed.

At 8:00 AM, Lou Skinner got out of his bed, took one glance out of the window to make sure it hadn't rained, and hit the shower. He thought to himself: The team should make the playoffs this year. I've got to make sure they get off to a good start this time. Must drill them hard on fundamentals. Need a deeper pitching rotation. With these thoughts going through his head, he stepped out of the shower, got dressed, and prepared himself for the Saturday morning Skinner ritual of going out for fresh rolls for the family.

Vinnie Panzini woke up at 8:15, as he smelled the pancakes being prepared by his mom for the Panzini household. What a great way to start the day, he thought.

The lights in the Gustafson, Dodsworth, Carson, and Jeffries homes, as well as those in the homes of the other team members, were all on by 8:30. The kids could walk to the field, but the parents were up anyway, to make sure their boys had the right breakfast and clothing.

With only Davey Filstein missing at the commencement of practice, Lou had the boys warm up their arms by throwing to each other. Then, he had them all gather around him at home plate for the initial pep talk.

"Guys, we had a disappointing season last year. Sure, there were teams worse than we were, and we beat some good teams along the way, but we should have finished higher. We were much too inconsistent. I will be stressing fundamentals more this time. At the beginning of any season, there's not too much hitting by any team. The one determining factor will be, which team throws the ball away less. I also want to remind you that there are no predetermined positions. I don't care what you did last year - good or bad. Everybody starts the season with a clean slate. For now, take these positions: Vinnie Panzini - catcher; George Porter - on the mound; Ronald Carson - first base; Nick Plugman and Donnie Bowman - second base; Joey Harrison and Marc Davidson - both go to shortstop; Ike Eichorn and Chris Conley - to third base; Al Gustafson - left field; Billy Jeffries - center field; Scott Edwards and Eddie Howe - right field.

Lou proceeded to put them through a vigorous workout, lasting almost an hour. When Davey Filstein arrived, Lou had him occupy shortstop, with Joey moving over to the pitcher's mound, George to first base, and Ronald to left field to alternate with Al. Things went pretty well. Lou liked what he saw, but he knew not to let the kids know it, lest they start relaxing.

The next hour was spent with batting practice, with Lou doing the pitching (to move things along). He started each kid off with slow stuff, working towards harder pitches eventually. Again, Lou was encouraged. The guys knew that Lou had two batting practice rules: Don't ask when/if you are up, and no one lays down on the field.

Since there were no new additions to the squad this year, Lou bypassed his usual first practice ritual of clocking each player's running speed, and decided to work on bunting, and bunting defense.

"The other teams bunted successfully on us too often last year, and unfortunately we couldn't return the favor," exhorted Lou. "The bunt can do a lot of things. It can get a hitter out of a batting slump, it can move runners along, it upsets the defense, and it ultimately draws the defense in a few steps, so there are more chances for a hitter who's swinging away to get it past the infielders."

Lou worked on their stances, their hand-positioning on the bat, and simultaneously worked with the fielders' positioning.

At the end of practice, Lou bellowed out, "OK, guys, good workout. See you same time next week. Pitchers, get ready to start throwing next time. Joey, Billy, and Ike, can I see each of you for a moment, please"?

After the others had headed towards their bikes or parents' cars, Lou Skinner spoke to the three boys. "Guys, you three are, in my mind, the leaders on this team. You're all talented, and the other boys look up to each of you. So, I'd like your opinions on what went wrong last year, and why we didn't do better than we did. After all, when I look at the other teams in our division, I don't see any with more talent, yet we couldn't finish higher than third. What's the answer?"

Ike Eichorn started forward, and said, "Mr. Skinner, I see two things wrong with the team, or at least, where we have to improve. One is our pitching depth. The top teams have three or four guys that can come in and get things done. We don't. With the rainouts that happen, we sometimes have to play three games in a week because of make-ups, and that's where we get hurt."

"Any ideas on who can pitch for us?" Lou chimed in.

"Yes," said Ike. "We know that George and Al are good, and Joey did a pretty good job, too, but I think the answer to our prayers is standing right next to me - Mr. Billy Jeffries."

Billy seemed stunned by Ike's statement, and took a few steps back while looking away. Apparently, this was the one thing he didn't want to hear.

"Billy, I happen to agree with Ike here," Lou said. "You have a strong and accurate arm in the outfield, or when I've put you anywhere else. What do you say; will you give it a try?"

"Well, I don't know, coach. I'm not sure I can do the job." At that moment, Billy's thoughts drifted back to several years ago when, at age nine, he had pitched in a game in another league (PAL), and although he'd started off like a ball of fire, striking out batter after batter, he suddenly hit three batters in a span of two innings, one of which was hurt really badly. That was the last time he ever pitched in a league game. However, he didn't want either Lou or his teammates to know he was scared to pitch, so finally he replied, "OK, maybe I'll give it a shot."

"Swell, Billy. Now, Ike, you said there were two problems you saw. What's the other?"

"Coach, I was talking to Dodsy the other day. When he told me our team batting average was .303, I couldn't believe it. Isn't that a low average for Little League, especially for a contender? We have good athletes. We should be hitting much higher, myself included. One of the guys on the Pirates was telling me that they go to the indoor batting cages a couple of times before the Spring season. Maybe we can do the same thing."

"Well, to tell you the truth, Ike, I don't like asking parents to shell out extra money for things like batting cages."

"But, coach," replied Joey. "Our parents are always giving us money for video games and stuff like that. I'm sure that wouldn't be a problem. Let's try it, OK?"

"Alright, boys. I'll call everyone's parents this week, but I'll make the batting cages optional. Anything you wish to add, Joey or Billy?"

Both of them shrugged their shoulders, and shook their head no.

"Alright boys, see you next week. Billy, be ready to pitch."

As the three boys walked towards their bikes, Billy turned to Ike and said, "Thanks a lot, Ike. I didn't hear you volunteering to pitch."

Joey interrupted. "Billy, you can do it. Ike was just complimenting you. I happen to agree with him."

"Well," replied Billy. "Some friend you are." At that, Billy jumped onto his bike and sped off.

"What's his story?" asked Ike.

"I don't know, Ike. I just don't know," said Joey

Joey called Paul Dodsworth as soon as he got home.

"What did Mr. Skinner want?" asked Paul. "Did he name you guys co-captains or something?"

Joey related the entire conversation they'd had with the coach, plus Billy's strange behavior and his riding off rather hurriedly.

"Well, if you want my opinion, Joey, Billy did what he did because he's afraid of failure. He's just insecure."

"But why, Dodsy? He's a great player. I'm sure he can be a great pitcher."

"Beats me, Joey. Anyway, want to do baseball cards this afternoon at my house, followed by a game of Strat-O-Matic?"

"OK, I'll be over at around 2 o'clock. See ya."

Chapter 8

Billy Jeffries came into house, slammed the front door, walked straight past his parents, and headed directly towards his bedroom.

"I wonder what's eating him," asked Mrs. Claire Jeffries.

"Who knows," replied Billy's Dad, Melvin Jeffries. "You know kids. Maybe something at the ball field."

"Mel, why don't you check up on him?"

Mr. Jeffries sauntered up to Billy's room, and rapped several times on the door before hearing a meek "come in" from Billy.

"What's up, son?"

"Nothing."

"Nothing? You call your actions nothing? Come on, Billy; you can talk to me. Did something happen at practice?"

"I really don't want to talk about it."

"You have to, son. Trust me, you'll feel better."

"Well, Dad, Joey and I got into a fight." Seeing his father become nervous, Billy quickly added, "Not a fist fight or anything like that. An argument."

"About what?"

"Nothing much."

"Billy, I know you prefer to keep things inside of you but I'm telling you, you'll feel a whole lot better if you can get it off your chest."

"OK, Dad. The coach asked me, Joey, and Ike to stay after practice to talk."

"Sort of a meeting of the minds?"

"Yeah, sorta."

"What about?"

"He called us the leaders of the team, and asked us how we thought we could become a better team. Ike and Joey said I should pitch."

"Well, what's wrong with that?"

"Dad, I'm afraid of overthrowing and hurting my arm for good. I don't want to pitch. I'm not comfortable doing it."

"Billy, you should feel honored that your teammates believe in you so much."

"Well, I don't, Dad. They can't make me do it. I won't do it."

"No, they can't force you to pitch. But, think it over."

"I'll think it over, but I know I won't change my mind."

That night, as Billy Jeffries lay in bed, bothered by not being able to level with his father, all he could picture were visual recollections of hitting batters, and their crying in pain. He had made his decision. He'd quit baseball before he'd ever pitch again.

Chapter 9

In the back of Lou Skinner's mind, as he led his squad through the next few practices, was getting a third and fourth solid pitching candidate. He knew he could probably get some quality innings out of Joey Harrison, but he really needed Joey as his shortstop, as well as being a back-up catcher for Vinnie Panzini. He figured on George Porter and Al Gustafson as his two sure starters, and assumed Billy Jeffries, being the great athlete he was, would easily slot in behind those two. Joey was already being counted on by Lou, so now he went through the process of letting anyone who wanted to throw from the mound, do so. Vinnie, Ronald Carson, and Chris Conley all tried, but even though outwardly Lou gave them encouragement, inside he knew that none of them would even be adequate. They either were too slow, too wild, looked uncomfortable, or were a mixture of all of the above.

"Billy, why don't you try the mound?" bellowed Lou.

"Er, coach, my arm hurts today. Maybe next practice."

At that point, Ronald Carson nudged Billy and said, "Billy, why are you lying about this? Your arm doesn't hurt. What's your story, man?"

Billy replied, "Nothing. Just leave me alone, will you, Ronald?"

Joey had been talking nearby to Dodsy on the sidelines, and went over to Billy.

"Hey, Billy. Sorry your arm hurts."

"Hello."

"What's wrong with you, Billy?"

"Nothing's wrong with me, Joey. Why is everyone on my case? Lay off, all of you." At that point, Billy moved away, rather hurriedly towards the outfield, where he proceeded to do some exercises, and then, as an errant ball made its way towards him, fired a perfect strike to the mound.

"Some sore arm," noted Ike Eichorn.

There was noticeable tension the rest of the practice, and Lou Skinner was in a sense happy to get the equipment into his car after it was over, and be on his way home.

Chapter 10

Finally, Opening Day was approaching. Saturday, after the ceremonies, it would be time to "Play Ball." Lou Skinner gave Paul Dodsworth a call, to go over the opening game starting lineup.

"Well, Dodsy, what do you think?" asked Lou.

"OK, Mr. Skinner, of course this is just my opinion, but I would go this way," answered Dodsy, and then proceeded to rattle off this order:

Nick Plugman	2B
Joey Harrison	SS
Billy Jeffries	CF
Ike Eichorn	3B
Vinnie Panzini	C
Al Gustafson	LF
George Porter	P
Scotty Edwards	RF
Ronald Carson	1B

As usual, Lou Skinner could not find any fault in Dodsy's order, so Lou replied, "Yeah we'll probably start off that way." Lou left it as being inconclusive, in the likely event the kids would be bugging Dodsy for the lineup. "Remind the guys to be there 11:45 on Saturday. We play the second game, right?"

"That's right," answered Dodsy. "Don't worry, we'll be there."

The kids had all received their uniforms at the last practice, and after the normal trading amongst some of the guys to accommodate sizes and lucky numbers, everything was set in Lou Skinner's mind, except for one thing: We need a deeper and more effective pitching staff. Why won't you pitch, Billy?

Chapter 11

Saturday came, and the weather was less than ideal for baseball. Although there was no threat of rain, the temperature figured to reach 55 degrees at the most, and there was a stiff breeze blowing. Joey's team, the Mets, were all at the field well before the 11:45 AM required time. By noon, as the opening day ceremonies were about to commence, the division Joey was in, the Majors, had all its league members - players and coaches, in full view of the parents of Springtown. Running out onto the field, team by team, were the Pirates, who were last year's champs, then the Reds, runners up to the Pirates, followed by the Mets, Dodgers, Indians, and Angels.

The first day's schedule of games was:
  Game One - Pirates vs. Indians
  Game Two - Mets vs Dodgers
  Game Three - Reds vs Angels
The Reds and Angels were free to go home following the ceremonies, since they were playing the third game, though decided to stay at the field and watch the first two contests. The Mets and Dodgers were able to alternatively use the practice field adjacent to the game field.

After the Mets had finished practice, they ambled over to the game field to watch the Pirates - Indians contest, now in the fourth inning, a game in which after the Indians had jumped out surprisingly in front 3-0, saw the Pirates storm back to take a safe 9-3 lead.

"Boy, the Pirates are going to be tough again this year, Dodsy," said Joey.

"Yeah, but you know what they say, baseball is a funny game," Dodsy replied.

The Pirates did, indeed, win their game from the Indians 13-4. The Pirates' star hitter and pitcher, Bruce Plank, went 3 for 4, including a long home run, and after overcoming some early wildness on his part, and some uncharacteristically sloppy fielding by his teammates, Plank settled down. When he left the mound after three innings, he was comfortably in front 11-3, striking out eight of a possible nine outs. Under the rules of this League, a pitcher could not pitch more than six innings in a calendar week (In the Springtown League, a calendar week was established as being Sunday through Saturday.). Therefore, Plank could technically pitch in both tomorrow's game against the Reds, and next Saturday's contest with the Dodgers, for a total of six innings maximum. (Had he pitched more than three innings today, he would have been required to refrain from pitching for at least 72 hours - another league rule - which was why Pirates manager Mike Plank, Bruce's father, lifted him after three innings, moving him to shortstop).

"Nice game, Bruce," said Joey Harrison, as the Pirates were leaving the field.

"Thanks, Harrison," replied Bruce Plank as he quickly ran off for a soda at the refreshment stand.

The Mets would be home team for their game against the Dodgers, so they practiced first. Georgie Porter, their pitcher for today, was warming up on the sidelines, and he felt good. But, as any player will tell you, from Little League all the way up to the Big Leagues, how you warm up often has nothing to do with how you play once "the bell rings." There are classic stories of professional pitchers who claimed they "had nothing" in warm-ups, and when the game began, they were unhittable. Of course, it's also worked in reverse. How many times have you read in the newspapers, where the catcher was quoted as saying,

"Man, he had great stuff and location warming up," only to see how lousy he was in the game?

As Game Two unfolded, this appeared to be one of those days where the pitcher was not as effective as he had been in warm-ups. The Dodgers were hitting a lot of hard shots; however, they were generally right at a fielder, plus there were a couple of great plays in the field, odd for an early season game. Nick Plugman made a leaping catch of a line drive to end the first inning, with runners on second and third. Then, in the top of the fourth, with the score knotted at 2-2, Dodger catcher and clean-up batter David Racine smacked a line drive to right-center field with two outs and the bases loaded, but Billy Jeffries made a superb running catch to end that threat.

In the bottom of the fourth, it seemed as though the Dodgers were emotionally down after having seen several opportunities to put the game away be wiped out by great and timely Met defense. Starting Dodger pitcher Ray Walker appeared to lose his concentration, and walked the first two batters. Then, with relatively light-hitting Ronald Carson up at the plate, a wild pitch moved the runners up to second and third. On a 2-2 pitch, Ronald lifted a foul pop up to first that was dropped by the Dodger first baseman. Given a new life, Ronald next hit a slow ground ball between short and third that he beat out for a hit, scoring one runner. Then, the floodgates opened. Nick Plugman walked, Joey Harrison singled in a run, Billy Jeffries doubled home two, and Ike Eichorn tripled in two more. By the time the inning was mercifully over, the Mets led 11-2. With that kind of lead, Lou Skinner took out George Porter from the mound, and Joey pitched the last two innings. Final score: Mets 12, Dodgers 4.

After the game, Lou reminded the players that this was only one game, and it was a lot closer than the final score indicated. Finally, he commented that it was defense that won the game for them. Tomorrow's game would be against the Angels, and then they'd meet the Reds and Pirates in that order.

"Hey, Vinnie, you'd better lay off all the pizza and stuff. We want you as quick as a cat behind the plate. You know those guys on the Reds and Pirates love to run," exhorted Al Gustafson.

"Would you guys cut it out, please," screamed Joey.

"Aw, was only kidding, Vinnie. Can't you take a joke?"

Vinnie looked straight into Al's eyes, and as a smile came slowly to his face, he replied, "Food is not a joking matter with me. Got it, pal?"

Chapter 12

The Mets won their next two games, beating the Angels 7-2, and the tough Reds 11-8. Now, it was time to face the Pirates. The defending champs were, like the Mets, undefeated so far, and they looked as formidable as last year. The Pirates, the Mets knew, would be the "team to beat."

Both teams had pitching restrictions today. Each club's ace, George Porter of the Mets and Bruce Plank of the Pirates, could only pitch three innings apiece today, as both had hurled three innings during the week.

As the game unfolded, both starting pitchers appeared to be at the top of their games. As a matter of fact, there was very little action in the first three innings, and as the "visiting" team, the Pirates, came up to the plate in the top of the fourth, Al Gustafson took the mound in a scoreless tie. Al had started and won his first game, against the Angels.

Al pitched reasonably well this time, but found himself on the short end of a 2-0 score, as the Mets came up in the bottom of the sixth and final inning. Vic Spurgen, the number two pitcher for the Pirates, had been sharp so far. But, with one out, substitute Chris Conley walked. Nick Plugman layed down a beautiful bunt down the third base line and beat it out for a hit. Joey Harrison was now up. Joey made a strong bid for a base hit, but his ground ball down the first base line was snagged by Pirate first baseman Bill Washington, who beat Joey to the bag on a bang-bang play. Two outs now, and with runners moving up to second and third, the tying run was now in scoring position for Billy Jeffries.

The Pirate manager, Mike Plank, called time and trotted to the mound, to talk to his players. In Mike's mind, there was the strategy of whether to pitch to

Billy or walk him, that had to be discussed. If they were to intentionally walk him and go against an unwritten "rule" of never putting the winning run on, it would bring up Ike Eichorn, certainly no slouch. They decided to pitch to Billy, although carefully.

The move didn't work out well for the Pirates, as Billy grounded a single to centerfield, scoring both runners to tie the game up. Ike followed with a single to left, but with the winning run on second, Vinnie Panzini flied out to center, sending the game into extra innings.

Joey Harrison now came into pitch. Joey had pitched against both the Dodgers and Angels in relief, and had been reasonably effective. This time, though, Joey didn't have it . The first two Pirate batters reached safely on singles, and that brought the dangerous Bruce Plank up to the plate. Wasting no time, he jumped on the first pitch and tripled over Eddie Howe's head in left field. Joey, bearing down, retired the next two Pirates on a strikeout and an infield pop-up, but then uncorked a wild pitch, Plank scoring. So, after retiring Billy Washington on a groundout, the Mets came up, needing three to tie the score.

Pitching for the Pirates now was Lenny Fielder, a big, hard throwing right hander. The Mets had Al Gustafson, Eddie Howe, and Donnie Bowman due up. The Met hitters were no match for the Pirate fireballer, Gustafson tapping out to the mound, and both Howe and Bowman striking out.

After the game, Lou Skinner talked to his boys, telling them that they'd played well, and would have other opportunities against the Pirates. He reminded them that they had come through big time in the sixth inning, tying up the game. He applauded the pitching and the defense, and in closing, told them not to get too down on themselves. It was only one game out of a long season.

Joey Harrison and Paul Dodsworth left together, being carpooled by Joey's parents. Both boys were silent on the way home. Joey kept thinking to himself: Why won't Billy pitch? What's he afraid of?

Chapter 13

The Mets rebounded in their next contest, against the Indians, winning handedly by a 10-2 score. The game afforded Lou Skinner an opportunity to experiment with a few other pitchers, to try and find a third quality hurler. Joey Harrison, Lou knew, was a real solid ballplayer, a good hitter and fielder, but Joey just did not have what it took as a pitcher against a strong hitting team like the Pirates, or even the Reds. The Mets would end their Spring season against these two teams, and obviously those games would have a tremendous bearing on the final standings. He knew he could count on George Porter and Al Gustafson, but who else, when the chips were down? "Billy, why won't you pitch?" muttered Lou again, sounding like a broken record.

As far as the Indians game was concerned, Lou let Vinnie Panzini pitch a little, since Nick Plugman was a capable back-up catcher (and there was always Joey who could go behind the plate as well, as he'd done in the past). But Vinnie, who Lou knew had a strong arm, was wild, and generally looked uncomfortable out there on the mound. He pitched to five batters, striking out the first one, then walking the next four. Although the Mets had a seemingly safe lead, Lou felt he had to make a change. "Who else can I put in?" said Lou.

Lou decided that Ike Eichorn would be the next logical candidate. Ike did an okay job, but Lou's conclusion was that Ike was no better as a pitcher than Joey, so in essence, this was nothing more than a trade off.

"Oh, well," whispered Lou, "maybe two pitchers can be enough if we can outhit and outscore the other teams." Lou, however, knew he was not being realistic. The Mets were a fairly solid hitting club, but not in the same "league" as

the lineup-loaded Pirates, and probably not even the Reds. Anyway, it promised
to be an interesting season.

Chapter 14

The Mets were victorious in their next three games, and entering their second meeting with the Pirates, the Mets record was 7-1. The Pirates were 8-0, and the Reds, the only other team mathematically in the race for either of the top two spots, were 6-2.

Standings were as follows:

Pirates 8 -0

Mets 7-1

Reds 6-2

Indians 2-6

Angels 1-7

Dodgers 0-8

That week, the Reds beat the Indians, which in itself was no surprise, except that the Indians gave them a real battle, until the Reds ultimately prevailed, 9-8. The Reds had by-passed their two top pitchers, Mitch Walters and Ryan Billigan, opting to save them for the Mets game. It was a calculated gamble, but it ultimately paid off.

So, as the Mets got ready to do battle with the Pirates, they knew the following: A win would tie them for first with the Pirates, but a loss would leave them tied for second with the Reds.

Lou Skinner felt he had to play the games one at a time. Georgie Porter would start, and depending on what unfolded, Lou would assess his options. The kids, Lou felt, had had a good practice this week, and were as ready as ever.

The Pirates were set with their pitching rotation. Mike Plank knew he'd go with his son Bruce as long as possible, with Vic Spurgen and Lenny Fielder both available.

Mike Plank didn't need a calculator to figure out the ramifications of this game. A victory for the Pirates mathematically assured them of finishing in first place for the first half of the season. A loss, and they'd have to beat the Dodgers and hope the Reds could upset the Mets this weekend.

An unusually large crowd was on hand for the weekday game, with parents of both the Pirates and the Mets scrambling home from work for the 6:00 PM starting time. They were treated to a good game.

Scoreless after two innings, the contest switched to more offense for the Mets in the third, as they put across two runs in that inning, on a double by George Porter, a walk to Ronald Carson, and consecutive two out singles by Joey, Billy, and Ike.

Georgie Porter was really on his game, and continued shutting out the Pirates. In the top of the fifth, the Mets pushed across another run, although you couldn't fault Pirate hurler Bruce Plank too much. Lead off batter Nick Plugman walked, and went to second on a passed ball. But Joey struck out, and Billy popped up. With two outs, another passed ball moved Nick to third. Ike, with a count of two balls and two strikes, grounded to first baseman Bill Washington, who bobbled the ball, allowing Ike to reach safely, with Nick scoring.

In the bottom of the fifth, with the Mets holding a 3-0 lead, George Porter gave up two singles, after having retired the lead off batter, bringing Bruce Plank to the plate. Plank continued to be "Mr. Clutch," driving a ball down the third base line for a double. One run scored, with the second runner trying to score all the way from first. However, Al Gustafson rifled a great throw to the plate from left field, Vinnie Panzini put the tag on, and the runner was out. Georgie went on to retire the next batter, Jason Satriano, on a ground ball back to the mound. The score now stood at 3-1, entering the sixth and final inning. After the Mets were retired in order in their half, Lou had a decision to make. Should he let Georgie finish the game, or bring in Al to pitch the sixth? Even if George made just one pitch in that inning, it would constitute a sixth inning of pitching, making him ineligible to pitch at all against the Reds. But, except for the brief rally by the Pirates in the fifth, George had been overpowering tonight. What if Al was ineffective? Who could he go to next against this robust Pirate lineup?

He decided to stick with George, and hoped that Al would turn in a complete game sparkler against the Reds, or that the Mets would do a lot of hitting this weekend.

Bill Washington led off for the Pirates, hoping to atone for his fifth inning error. He carefully worked the count to three and one. George felt Washington would look over the next pitch in the hopes of drawing a walk and thus bringing the tying run to the plate, and he "grooved" the next pitch, just trying to get a strike. But, the Pirates didn't earn their reputation as an aggressive ballclub for nothing. Washington, swinging from the hips, laced the pitch over the right field fence for a home run.

This seemed to unnerve George, who proceeded to walk the next two batters. Lou had no choice but to relieve George with Al.

After his warmups, Al got ready to face the Pirates. He appeared sharp, and retired the next two batters, the first on a called third strike, the next on a popup to Ronald Carson. That brought up lead off batter Eric Stein and Al, perhaps trying to overthrow, unleashed a wild pitch, placing runners on second and third. A single would at least tie up the game, and possibly win it for the Pirates.

"Come on, Gusto," yelled a nervous Paul Dodsworth from the dugout.

The next two pitches to Stein were both fouled off, followed by two pitches out of the strike zone. Full count, with Vic Spurgen on deck and Bruce Plank to follow.

Stein then reached for a pitch targeted for the outside corner of the plate and lifted a foul ball down the first base line that Ronald Carson couldn't reach. The next pitch was not where Al wanted it, and Stein sent a hard line drive near third that had base hit written all over it. But Ike Eichorn speared the hot smash, and the game was over. The Mets had hung on to win it, 3-2. Lou Skinner breathed a sigh of relief, but like most good managers, he had already turned his thoughts towards the Reds Game. At best, he had Al for five innings on the mound. No Georgie Porter, and unfortunately, no Billy Jeffries.

Chapter 15

It was Friday, and tomorrow was to be the big weekend, the end of the season's first half. The Pirates and the Mets were tied for first place, each sporting 8-1 records. The Reds were a game back at 7-2. The Dodgers, Indians, and Angels were mathematically eliminated from playoff contention for the first half season, but because of the uniqueness of the Springtown Little League, every team would start over again in September, all with an equal chance, at least mathematically, of finishing in the top two spots.

Individual honors would also be at stake this weekend, leading to All Star berths, plus, when all was said and done, playing the game itself was something all kids wanted to do, and the coaches and managers all realized, or should have anyway, that the main purpose in being out there was to have fun. Again, there had never been a Springtown season where the same two teams finishing "in the money" in the first half repeated the deed in the second half. One team, perhaps, but never both. This kept the spirits up on all the teams.

Paul Dodsworth was munching on an apple during lunch period at school, and although to a casual observer Paul appeared to be studying for an exam, he was in fact going over the team's stats.

"Hey, Dodsy," yelled out Vinnie Panzini, "come over here."

"Forget it, Vinnie, I've already eaten my sandwich, so I've got nothing for you," Paul replied as he walked over to Vinnie.

"Hey, man, I don't want your lunch. Well, I do, but I can't take what you don't have, so let's get down to business. Who's making the All Star team this year?"

"How would I know," said Dodsy, "that's up to Mr. Skinner."

"C'mon, Dodsy. I know he communicates with you between games on the phone."

"Yeah, he does, but never to discuss All Stars. Besides, shouldn't you be worrying about the Reds?"

"Look, you're supposed to be good with facts, Dodsy, so let's examine this:

1. We just beat the Pirates.
2. We've already beaten the Reds.
3. The Reds almost lost to the Indians.
   "Don't worry about the game."

"Maybe you're right, Vinnie, but you know me; I always worry."

"You're a good guy, Dodsy. I don't know if I'd have your enthusiasm if I weren't playing."

"Vinnie, I came to terms with my ability, or rather my lack of it, a long time ago. I'm content with being the best statistician I can be. Understand?"

"Yeah, sure, Dodsy. Take it easy. Chill out. Anyway, I gotta go. I'll see you on Sunday."

Chapter 16

The Pirates had the Saturday game, and easily defeated the Dodgers, 15-5. Now, on Sunday, several members of the Pirates were on hand to watch the Mets-Reds contest, and the possibilities were as follows:

1. A Mets win and they'd finish tied for first with the Pirates. The only tie breaker would be head to head competition, but since the teams split their two games, they'd be forced to play a one game playoff next week. The winner would be declared the first half champs, the loser garnering second place.

2. A Mets loss and the Pirates would clinch the first half championship. The Mets and Reds would both finish at 8-2, setting up a one game playoff for second.

The Mets would be the visiting team today, and they had Al Gustafson pitching, for a maximum of five innings. The Reds would counter with their ace, Mitch Walters, with Ryan Billigan available for as long as necessary.

Last time the teams faced each other, there had been a lot of scoring, but Lou Skinner knew very well how tough both Walters and Billigan could be. Lou hoped Al would be sharp, and that the Mets would be comfortably in front by the sixth inning.

The Mets did indeed start out of the gate well, and on singles by Joey Harrison, Billy Jeffries, and Ike Eichorn, they jumped out in front 1-0. At the same time, Al Gustafson was incredibly sharp on the mound, and the only base runner the Reds had was via a two out walk to Neil Golden in the second inning, who was left stranded.

The Mets appeared to make things safer for themselves in the top half of the fourth, pushing across two more runs to take a 3-0 advantage. In the bottom of the fourth, Al breezed his way through the Reds' 2-3-4 batters, striking out two and getting the other out via a weak tap back to the pitcher's mound.

As the teams got ready for the top of the fifth, the skies opened up and it began to rain heavily. Equipment was packed up, and everyone ran for shelter. It was an official game, and could be "called" by the home plate umpire if the rain didn't abate.

The Reds stood helplessly by, under the roof of the refreshment stand, as the rain continued to come down, and after 20 minutes, the prospects for play resumption were not good.

Just then, however, the sun came out and the rain ended, and with the ump's chant of "Play Ball," the Mets and Reds were ready to resume.

It would have seemed difficult to an impartial observer to figure out which team actually had the lead, since the Mets couldn't wait to get back onto the field, while the Reds, getting a tremendous break in that the game would be continued, appeared lethargic and uninterested. Perhaps it was the thought of continuing to face Al Gustafson again when Al was as sharp as could be. Maybe too, there was a feeling amongst the Red players, at least subliminally, that the Mets were only a hit or two away from already having made the margin much larger than three runs.

Pete Billigan, Reds manager, couldn't help but sense his team's emotion, or rather their lack of it. He addressed them this way: "Look, guys, I know we haven't hit Gustafson today, but he can only go five innings, so let's keep it close and see what happens. They can't bring in Porter either. Remember, baseball is a funny game. We're a good team, and so are the Mets, so let's go out there fighting." The team put collective hands together, and emitted a resounding "Let's go" shout.

Pete Billigan knew he had played on his team's psyche just right. No use telling them they would clobber Gustafson, who was pitching the game of his life so far, but he knew whoever the Mets brought in for the sixth would be a welcome sight for his team. His speech, he hoped, would get them through the fifth inning at no worse than a three run deficit.

But, the fifth inning continued to look familiar. The Mets loaded the bases with one out, and Ike Eichorn was up. Lou Skinner was hoping this would lead to a minimum of two more runs, which would give him some breathing room in the last inning, when Gustafson had to come out. In the opposition dugout, Pete Billigan knew he was on the verge of having to take his pitcher, Mitch Walters, out, and bring in his son Ryan to relieve.

"C'mon, Ike," yelled Paul Dodsworth from the bench, hoping to pencil some more runs into the scorebook.

On a 2-1 pitch from Billingan, Ike, although swinging a tad late, hit a hard ground ball between first and second. A certain hit and two RBI's, but wait! The runner on first, Billy Jeffries, had no time to react, and the batted ball hit him in the leg. This meant that the runners on third and second had to go back to their bases, the runner Billy was out, Ike replacing him on first. It was of little consolation to Ike that according to the rule book, a batted ball that directly hits a runner is technically scored as a base hit.

Vinnie Panzini, the next batter, sent a long fly ball to left-center field that Mitch Walters, now the center fielder after having been relieved, made a fine running catch on. Three outs. The Mets couldn't believe it. Three runners on, their power hitters up, two hard hit balls resulting, and nothing, absolutely nothing to show for it. The funny game of baseball wasn't so funny to Lou Skinner and his squad at the moment. Lou had to pray that Al Gustafson could continue his mastery for one more inning, and that the sixth inning reliever (at this point, leaning towards Joey) could hold the Reds down.

Al was dynamite again in the fifth, mowing down the Reds 1-2-3. He was heart-broken to know he couldn't finish the game, especially since he had not allowed a hit, but rules were rules, and there was nothing Al or Lou could do about it.

Lou exhorted his team on, but you could sense it in the air, the Mets were through scoring runs today. Gustafson, Donnie Bowman, and Chris Conley went out in order.

Joey took his warm up tosses in the bottom of the sixth, and he knew he had to have his control. The eighth and ninth place hitters were the first two due up for the Reds, and he didn't want to issue any bases on balls.

But sometimes this is easier said than done. You can lose your concentration, or you can be concentrating too hard. In any event, Joey was doing something wrong, because he walked both batters, bringing the tying run to the plate in the person of Steven Rourke. Joey got the first pitch over for a strike, and with the next one, induced Rourke to ground it between short and third. But, for some strange reason, Nick Plugman was late in covering second base for a would-be force play, and so Ike Eichorn had to redirect his throw to first, a hurried throw at that, forcing Chris Conley, subbing for Ronald Carson, to come off the bag. All runners were safe.

Plugman momentarily redeemed himself on the next play, flagging down Brian Sumner's hard grounder and throwing him out at first. One out, one run in, and runners on second and third. Ryan Billigan up. Joey worked carefully, but after Billigan fouled off several 3-2 pitches, Joey ultimately walked him.

Joey did retire Mitch Walters next, but it wasn't easy. First, a wild pitch scored the lead runner, with the others moving up a base. Then, a fierce line drive back to the box, which Joey luckily speared for out number two.

What a game this was turning into! 3-2 Mets, two outs, runners on second and third. Seth Kammawitz up now for the Reds. Lou called time, and went out to talk to Joey. They discussed their options:

1. Walk Kammawitz to set up a force at any base.
2. Pitch to him.
3. Relieve Joey with Ike.

The decisions were to stick with Joey, also not to walk the batter. The reason for not walking him was that a subsequent walk to the following batter would force in a run. Joey's control was not that great today, and there figured to be less pressure pitching to Kammawitz.

But, pitching with less pressure was one thing. Getting the batter out would be another.

Joey got the first pitch over, and breathed a little easier. An outside pitch, a foul ball, and a high pitch out of the strike zone produced a 2-2 count. Joey poised himself on the rubber, reared back and threw a great pitch on the outside corner that Kammawitz fought off somewhat defensively, resulting in a tap towards the first base side of the mound. Joey raced over for the ball, but slipped on the rain wettened grass, and had to throw from his knees. Joey couldn't get a good grip on the ball, also wet, and it sailed past Chris Conley at first. Two runs scored, and the incredulous but jubilant Reds were jumping up and down, screaming and yelling their lungs out.

The Mets were in a collective state of shock. They couldn't believe what had happened. Joey was at the end of the bench, practically crying. Billy went over to Joey, put his arm around him, and tried his best to console his friend. As the rest of the team sat on the bench, heads down, awaiting a talk from Lou, Joey looked Billy in the eye and asked, "Billy, why won't you pitch?"

Billy stared back at his buddy, and after a moment of hesitation, whispered back, "I can't, Joey. Please don't ask me again."

Lou's speech was a long one, because he had to get his troops thinking in a positive frame of mind. He told them how well they had played today, that the last play wasn't Joey's fault, and on a dry playing surface, Joey could make that play in his sleep. He refreshed their memories about Ike's ground ball that had struck Billy and how the game seemed to turn on that play.

Now, for the business at hand. A one game playoff next Saturday against the Reds. The winner would finish the first half in second place, behind the Pirates. The loser would be shut out of first half playoff recognition. Before leaving, Lou brought up the great game Al had pitched, and that if they could beat the Reds next week, today's loss would be a faded memory.

"But Mr. Skinner," said George Porter, "if we'd have won today, we would have been tied for first with the Pirates, with a one game playoff for first. Now that's gone."

"Yeah, even if we would have wound up losing to the Pirates, we'd still have finished in second automatically," chimed in Scotty Edwards.

"True, boys," replied Lou, "but there's no use crying over spilled milk. Let's have a good practice this week, and get the Reds on Saturday. Okay?"

"Okay," said the boys in unison, but not wholeheartedly. This was a tough loss, Lou knew, so at this point it would be best to drop it and let time heal wounds. No rah-rah stuff for now. Baseball, like life itself, could be a humbling experience.

Chapter 17

Next Saturday couldn't come soon enough for the Mets. Every time team-mates ran into each other in or out of school, it conjured memories of last week-end's incredible loss. Lou Skinner's pep talk after the game apparently did little to help. Joey couldn't talk about the game, which was totally inconsistent with his personality. Vinnie was looking for anyone to start a fight. Al Gustafson was in no mood for the girls. Chris Conley spent the greater part of the week walk-ing with his head down. Even Paul Dodsworth, the walking statistician, knew it would be a waste of time to bring stats to school (He compiled them of course, but kept them at home).

Lou's decision to hold practice Friday night was smart. Had it been earlier this week, he would have been working with zombie-like players. By Friday, they seemed to be out of their funk, much like getting over a virus.

Joey was still a little down on himself, but the guys went out of their way to make him know they weren't faulting him for the loss. Lou was prepared to remind the boys that the game should have never come down to one final play, and that they had had ample opportunities to break it open, only to see a mix-ture of bad luck and non-clutch offense take over. But, Lou never had to say a word about it. This was a determined bunch of boys he was observing at practice today.

Finally, the day of the game approached. The Reds won the coin toss, and would be the home team. Is my club really ready to go? wondered Lou.

Both teams were solid with pitching today. The Reds would start Mitch Walters, and Lou was going back with Al Gustafson. Georgie Porter was the Mets' ace, but Gustafson had been incredible last time out, and the move couldn't really be questioned.

As it turned out, Al wasn't nearly as sharp as last week, but with the way the Mets were hitting today, it didn't seem to matter. They say hitting can be contagious; if so, the Mets had the sports equivalent of "strep throat" today. When capable but light-hitting Nick Plugman started off the game with a double in the left-center field gap, you could sense this was going to be the Mets' day. Joey singled, so did Billy, followed by a triple by Ike. Before the top of the first inning was completed, the Mets had six runs for Al to work with.

By the fifth inning, with Mitch Walters long gone from the mound and the Mets comfortably in front 10-4, Lou relieved Al with Georgie, who was sharp enough. When subs Davey Filstein and Chris Conley delivered two out RBI's apiece in the sixth, the contest was no longer in doubt, and when Georgie recorded the final out of the game with a strikeout, the score stood at 18-5. What a difference a week had made.

Lou decided to employ some reverse psychology on the boys this time (Remember, the league was in recess until the second half would begin in September).

"Boys, listen up. Great game today, but we've still got a long way to go. We could easily be out of the Championship Series unless we improve certain facets of our game. We came close to finishing first this half, but just as close to being out of contention. I'll remind you of something else. Since this league developed the first half/second half format, there hasn't been one time where the same teams finished first and second in both halves. If the Pirates finish first again and we don't finish second, we've got to struggle just to get to the Championship Series. Enjoy the victory today, but over the summer, stay in shape and be focused on what we still have to accomplish. I'll be in touch with each of you over the summer, as soon as I get the schedule for the second half. We'll probably have a few weeks' worth of practices before the opener. Have a great summer, boys."

As the team made its way towards the parking lot, Ike and Joey were walking together. Ike recalled to Joey the time Lou Skinner had spoken to Billy and the two of them before the season.

"You know something, Joey, not much has changed since that day. You and me are not exactly setting the world on fire as pitchers, and it doesn't look like we'll get any help from outside sources, if you know what I mean."

"I know what you mean, Ike. Billy's been my best friend for a long time, but now he seems like a stranger to me. I not only can't talk to him about pitching, I just can't seem to talk to him about anything."

"Guess you and I better get some special vitamins for arms, Joey."

"Yeah, well, I'll see ya, Ike," Joey said as he spotted his parents' car and he headed off in that direction.

Chapter 18

That night, at around 2:00 AM, Billy Jeffries awoke from his sleep. He'd been having a nightmare. This one was crystal clear, at least insofar as the images were concerned. There was a big room, with a line down the middle, much like a half court line in a basketball arena. On one side were Billy's Met teammates. On the other side was Billy, looking down at a little boy. The boy, about nine years of age, was wearing a batting helmet. He was lying on the floor, holding his left shoulder, obviously in a lot of pain. Next to the boy was a baseball, with smoke appearing to come out of it. It was at this juncture that Billy opened his eyes.

Now, Billy sat up in his bed. Not only did he know he'd have trouble getting back to sleep, he wondered how long he'd have to continue being tormented by something that had happened years ago. Would he be forced to quit baseball, the game he loved?

Chapter 19

The summer vacation period meant different things to each of the guys. For Billy, it was a drive down to North Carolina with his family to visit relatives. For Dodsy, it was going up to Canada, with a stop on the way home at Cooperstown, New York, home of the Baseball Hall Of Fame. Joey and his family spent two weeks at Cape Cod. Al had to fend off the advances of girls he met while with his folks on Virginia Beach (not that he minded it). Vinnie's father had vacation time over Christmas, so he stayed in the neighborhood, checking out the new pizza place, and giving them suggestions for improvement. Ike went to a basketball camp, along with Nick. Ronald was a counselor in training at a toddlers' day camp.

Of course, when the whole team reassembled with Lou for practice in late August, everyone agreed that the summer had gone by too fast. The subject quickly turned to baseball, and the fact that the Indians had picked up a new player, Wally Seedman, who'd just moved to the area. The kid was supposed to be a fantastic athlete, and a pitcher to boot. He'd transform them into instant contenders.

The Mets, Lou informed them, wouldn't have to wait long to find out. They opened in two weeks against the Indians.

Lou decided to treat this first practice as if it had been five months off instead of just two. That is, he started on basics again: building up the strength in their arms, lots of fungo popups, and, of course, normal fielding and hitting practice. The technical stuff, like hitting the cutoff man, protecting in the field against an opponent's attempt at a first and third double steal, and bunting would follow in succeeding workouts.

Lou's feelings about the team hadn't changed. It was a good club, solid and deep. It could go all the way. But, it was also a team in a highly competitive league, which had a playoff system that taxed a squad's pitching staff, unless your number one and two hurlers were "on" each game. The playoffs, you see, worked a little differently vs. the regular season. The restriction was that a kid could throw a maximum of six innings every two games. For example, if a team had playoff games on Saturday and Sunday of one weekend, a pitcher could go four innings on Saturday and come back to throw two more innings the next day. This was in contrast to the regular season, where if you threw up to three innings, you had to wait 24 hours to pitch again, and if you threw more than three but no more than five, the waiting period was 72 hours, plus a maximum six innings in a calendar week Sunday through Saturday.

Lou knew his options: Bank exclusively on Georgie and Al in the playoffs, which he was already guaranteed of their being in, due to their first half second place position, or focus on improving a third pitcher (Joey or Ike, it appeared). The first option wasn't too realistic, and he was aware that he had his work cut out for him with pitcher #3. Joey and Ike were real good ballplayers, but Lou had his doubts about either of them on the mound during crunch time. Of course, he kept his feelings to himself.

Lisa Skinner told her husband over dinner one night to "lighten up" a little. "It's not like you to be so perturbed about these kids, honey."

"I know, Lisa, it's just that this year, I think we've got a real shot at the championship."

"Well, you haven't lost it yet."

"Lisa, good managers are always looking ahead."

"Gotcha, hon. Now, let's get dinner out of the way, so we can take the kids over to the park, okay?"

"You got it!!"

Chapter 20

The Mets got to the field a little earlier than usual on "re-opening" day, anxious to get started again, and curious about the Indians' Wally Seedman.

Their curiosity turned to frustration once the game began, as Seedman struck out four of the first six Mets he faced, and didn't allow a base runner until Ronald walked in the third inning.

As the game entered the fourth inning, the score was 0-0, as Georgie was equally brilliant on the mound for the Mets.

Finally, the Mets' bats woke up in the bottom of the inning, starting with a beautiful bunt single by Joey, who took second on the overthrow to first by the Indians' third baseman.

Billy dug in against Seedman, and as he'd done so many times before, came through. This time he laced a double down the third base line to score Joey with the game's first run. Billy then took took third on a wild pitch with Ike at the plate. Ike lifted a fly ball to center which, although caught, plated Billy via a sacrifice fly. 2-0, Mets. Vinnie grounded out to short, and Al bounced back to the mound, ending the inning, but the Mets felt good about their bats starting to come alive, and of course, taking the lead.

With the relatively weak Dodgers on the Mets' imminent schedule, and Georgie having already gone four innings, Lou decided to let Georgie go one more inning and see what was going to happen. If he had to use Al for one or two innings, he could use him again for the next game, then finish up with Joey or Ike, or if necessary, Georgie.

The strategy worked. Georgie continued his brilliance, and in the last of the fifth, the Mets literally squeezed home an insurance run. Georgie walked, stole second, went to third on a ground out to second by Donnie, and easily scored on a beauty of a squeeze bunt by Chris, which made Lou especially proud. Chris had been having a rough year at the plate, but had been working a lot on his bunting lately. Today, it really paid off.

Lou, explaining to an understanding Georgie about his strategy, had Al go out to pitch the sixth inning. Al's first three pitches were balls, making Lou a little nervous, but then Al settled down and, aided by a great play in the hole by Ike for the third out, preserved the shutout and the win.

After the game, the Mets were unanimous in their praise of the Indians's Wally Seedman. There was a feeling that Seedman could knock off the Reds or Pirates at some point this year.

That night, Joey invited Billy to his house. Joey knew that the relationship between the two was not what it once had been, and he was determined to do everything he could to get it back on track. They rented a movie, and they both enjoyed it a lot. Billy seemed like his old self, which meant a lot of joking around. When Billy's father came to pick him up, he sensed that his son had not looked this happy in months. Joey felt the same way, and later realized that the subject of baseball had not come up once. Strange, thought Joey. Two lovers of the game, and not a word spoken about it. Oh well, opined Joey, I can always call Dodsy for my "fix,", which is what he did.

Chapter 21

As the second half of the season progressed, it appeared to be a four team race amongst the Pirates, Reds, Indians, and Mets. The Pirates, although winning with regularity, didn't seem to care as much as usual, plus they were experimenting a lot with their lineup, knowing they'd won the first half, and were automatically in the playoffs. The Reds, on the other hand, just missed out on one of the first half playoff spots, so they were treating each second half contest as a matter of life and death. The Indians, still longshots even with the addition of Wally Seedman, were also playing inspired ball. The Mets wanted to at least finish second again, meaning that should the Pirates repeat, the Reds and Indians would be eliminated from postseason competition. If the Mets and either the Reds or Indians were the top two teams this half, the team that wasn't there would be gone, and of course, the Pirates still had the first half sewn up.

So, as the second half season was winding down to the last two weeks, and each team had three games remaining, the records stood as follows:

Pirates 5-2, with games left against the Reds, Angels, and Indians

Mets 5-2, playing the Angels, Dodgers, and Reds

Reds 5-2, playing the Pirates, Indians, and Mets

Indians 4-3, playing the Dodgers, Reds, and Pirates

The Dodgers and Angels were too far behind for playoff contention, but hoped to play the spoiler's roles.

The Reds obviously had the toughest schedule remaining, playing each of the other contenders, while the Indians knew they could not count completely on Wally Seedman for both the Reds and Pirates, since the games both fell into the same calendar week.

Chapter 22

The "plot" really thickened that Saturday when the Reds upset the Pirates, and the Mets and Indians both won.

Here were the complete standings:

Mets 6-2

Reds 6-2

Pirates 5-3

Indians 5-3

Dodgers 1-7

Angels 1-7

The following Tuesday, the Indians squared off against the Reds, and as indicated earlier, the former were clearly in the midst of a dilemma. They had to still play the Pirates on Saturday. How should they handle their pitching rotation? It was decided to go with Seedman now, since unless they could catch up with either the Reds or Mets in the standings, the Indians would be mathematically eliminated anyway.

Seedman was his usual brilliant self, but after four innings, the Indians trailed the Reds 1-0, and it didn't get any better after that. Three Indian errors in the fifth inning opened up the floodgates, and when the Indians took the field in the top of the sixth, they were on the short end of a 4-0 score, and Seedman was out of the game, which meant he could at least pitch one inning against the Pirates.

The game ended 6-1, Reds. The Indians now had four losses, and would be officially eliminated from the playoffs if the Mets were to win at least one of their remaining contests, or if the Pirates won both of their clashes. The Reds, meanwhile, by virtue of today's victory, could finish the second half no worse than tied for second.

The Mets played Thursday night against the Dodgers, one night after the Pirates knocked off the Angels. Lou had Al on the mound, with Georgie braced for Sunday's game against the Reds. Lou had two wishes tonight: One, of course, was a win; the other being an easy win at that, so he could remove Al from the hill early and have him as an insurance policy on Sunday.

Lou's prayers were answered. The Mets' bats were alive, and due largely to home runs by Ike and Vinnie, they led 9-1 after three innings. Lou thus brought in Joey to pitch the fourth, and although he struggled a little, he was able to finish the game, and the Mets were victorious, 15-4. Everything seemed to be falling into place nicely for Lou's squad.

Saturday, the Indians and Pirates squared off. Incredibly, after five innings, the game was deadlocked at 4-4. In the top of the sixth, Wally Seedman stepped up to the plate. Although the Indians were now out of possible post-season contention, they were still playing for pride. Seedman, the complete ballplayer, smashed a 2-0 pitch over the fence for a two run homer, and then proceeded to take the mound for the bottom of the sixth. 1-2-3, he retired the side. The Pirates and Indians ended the second half with records of 6-4.

The Mets and Reds both had a lock on the second half playoffs; it was only a matter of who would finish first.

As Sunday arrived, the Reds had their ace, Mitch Walters, pitching against Georgie. Pete Billigan's Reds squad was the home team today.

The Mets started out quickly against Walters. Nick walked, Joey had a bunt single, and after Billy lined out to short, Ike singled up the middle, scoring Nicky and sending Joey to third. But Walters then got tough, striking out Vinnie swinging, and Al looking.

The Reds scratched out a run in the second off Georgie on a lead off pop fly double by the hustling Seth Kammawitz, and consecutive ground outs to Nick.

It stayed deadlocked at 1-1 through four innings, but in the top of the fifth, the Mets broke through against Walters for two runs, with the bench coming up big. Eddie Howe drew a leadoff walk and reached second base on a wild pitch. Chris bunted, and not only advanced Eddie to third, but beat it out for a base hit. After Chris stole second, putting runners on second and third with nobody out, Marc Davidson grounded to the left side of the mound. Mitch Walters made a great play in knocking the ball down, and was able to get the out at first, but Eddie scored the go-ahead run, Chris taking third.

The Met bench was alive, and both Eddie and Marc received congratulations upon returning to the dugout. The subs all year had accepted their roles and continued to practice hard, and now it was paying off.

At this time, Pete Billigan brought his son Ryan in to relieve Walters. Joey was up now for the Mets, but on a foul ball off his bat, Brian Sumner made a great catch, and Chris couldn't advance. However, Billy singled up the middle, sending Chris in, before the inning ended with Ike grounding out.

One of baseball's foremost cliches is that it's "a game of inches,", which became visible in the bottom of the fifth. With one out, the Reds' Neil Golden walked, and Brian Sumner followed with a single. Ryan Billigan was up, and on the first pitch, Vinnie couldn't handle the ball in the dirt, moving runners up to second and third. Billigan then grounded a shot down the first base line, and Chris missed coming up with it by that proverbial "inch.". Moreover, Chris was a lefty. Had Ronald, a righty, been at first, there's a good chance he would have come up with it. So, instead of two outs, one run in, and a runner on third, it was one out, two runs in, and a runner on second.

Georgie, pitching tough, got the equally tough Mitch Walters on a pop-up to Joey at short, but Seth Kammawitz singled to left center, scoring Billigan. 4-3, Reds.

The side was finally retired, and now the Mets were up in the sixth. The inning, the game, and the second half of the season were over before they knew what had hit them. On just five pitches from Billigan, the Mets were out in order.

The jubilant Reds were thus the second half champs, the Mets finishing second again. Lou told the boys that as soon as he knew the playoff format, he'd let them know. He told the boys to keep their chins up, that they could just as easily have won each half, and that they had the playoffs to look forward to.

Chapter 23

At a league meeting shortly thereafter, Lou learned that the playoff schedule would work this way: Because the Pirates' win/loss record in their first half championship (9-1) was better than that of the Reds' second half record (8-2), the Pirates were awarded a first round bye, even though the Reds' collective record of 16-4 was superior to that of the Pirates, who were 15-5. Actually, even the Mets had the same record total as the Pirates, but League officials had a list of "tie breakers" to determine the format each year, since the split season had been established and it clearly stated that if a team's record in either half was superior, they would be given the edge.

So, it would be the Mets and the Reds squaring off in a best two out of three semi-final round, the winner meeting the Pirates in the Championship Series. The Reds would be the home team in Game One, and if necessary, in Game Three.

Game One was slated for Wednesday night. The Mets worked out on Tuesday afternoon. Lou tried to rationalize what Sunday's loss to the Reds had meant. On the one hand, even if the Mets had won, it would still have been the same two ball clubs squaring off in the semis, due to that tie-breaker rule, only that the Mets would have been home team twice. That in itself was no big deal; however, psychologically, the Reds had to have the upper hand now, after pulling off the hard-fought win.

Lou, sensing his team felt like second-class citizens, reminded them that they had trounced the Reds 18-5 in the first half one game playoff for second place, which had followed on the heels of that traumatic 4-3 loss, when Joey had slipped on the grass and had thrown the ball away.

Talk was one thing, though, action another. How would the playoffs un-fold? It was anybody's guess.

Chapter 24

As Wednesday rolled around, the talk in school was centered on who would pitch for the Mets today. Mostly everybody figured it would be Georgie, their ace. But Dodsy, who had discussed the rotation with Lou at practice, knew he was leaning towards Al. Gusto's masterpiece against the Reds earlier this season, when he was absolutely unhittable before leaving the contest after five innings, had stuck in Lou's mind. Either way, Lou couldn't go too wrong, as both pitchers had had great seasons. The problem could arise once they got to the second line pitchers, where neither Joey or Ike had proven over the season that they could do the job against stiff competition.

Lou, conscious of possibly deflating Al's or Georgie's egos, decided to talk to both of them as soon as they arrived at the field. He spoke to George first. Georgie was very flexible, and that made it easier for Lou.

"Look, Mr. Skinner, I know I'm going to get my chance also. I'll be ready when you need me."

"You know, Georgie, that's very mature of you. To tell you the truth, I'm not sure who to start myself. After all, both of you guys are great pitchers."

After talking to both Georgie and Al, he decided on starting Al today. One thought popped into his head in making the decision: Yes, Georgie was unusually mature and gracious about it, but he gave in a little too easily, and maybe, just maybe, he wasn't mentally ready to start today.

Chapter 25

So, it was to be Al Gustafson against Mitch Walters. Both pitchers were sharp in the early going, but with the Reds "breaking the ice" in the second inning, they entered the third inning leading 1-0.

With two outs in the third, Chris walked, and Nick blooped a single to right. Joey came through, singling to center and Chris, running all the way with two outs, scored to tie up the game. Walters, hanging tough, got Billy out on a fly to center.

The score remained 1-1 going into the bottom of the fourth, when Al uncharacteristically walked the first two batters. Lou began pacing back and forth in the dugout. A manager hates more than anything to see walks. Besides obviously putting runners on base, the defense has a tendency to let down, even in a playoff game. This came to light when the next batter blooped a ball to left field that Donnie had to go a considerable distance for, and although Donnie got to the ball, it dropped out of his glove. It was scored a hit, but Donnie was normally a sure-handed fielder wherever Lou put him, and that was a play he usually made.

The runners had to hold up in case the ball had been caught, so they could only advance one base each. Now, the bases were loaded with no one out, and Steven Rourke, the Reds' leadoff batter today, was up. Al paused on the mound, trying to compose himself. He then proceeded to rear back and fire three straight strikes past Rourke. One out, Brian Sumner up. Lou called time, visited the mound, and told Al, "Give him nothing but heat. If you tire, I can bring in Georgie next inning. Let's work out of this now." Al nodded his head, took a deep breath, and went to work on the batter. With the count two balls and two strikes, Al threw a beauty over the outside corner of the plate, and when the umpire bellowed, "Strike three," the Mets players on and off the field, as well as their parents and friends, went nuts.

"One more to go, Gusto," yelled Dodsy. That one more, though, was Mitch Walters, a tough, tough hitter. Lou felt that if Walters put the ball in play, he still would not be able to pull it against Al, who was throwing bullets now. He had Joey shade towards the second base bag, and told Nicky to position himself two steps more towards first base than normal. Lou looked like a genius when Walters hit a hot grounder between first and second that Nicky was able to get to, and throw Walters out at first.

Walters somehow was able to compose himself enough to refrain from throwing his helmet in disgust, which would have meant automatic ejection from the game.

The Mets' bench was alive now, and when Ike and Vinnie led off the fifth with back to back singles, it looked real good for Lou's squad. Mitch Walters was then visited at the mound by manager Pete Billigan, to try to calm his pitcher down.

Gusto was up for the Mets, and Lou tried to surprise the Reds by calling for a bunt. But the bunt by Al was hit too hard, Walters fielding it and easily throwing to third for the force play. When Donnie and Scotty both struck out, the inning, which had started so promisingly, was over.

In the bottom of the fifth, Al was still on the mound, but perhaps the fourth inning events had taken something out of him, because Seth Kammawitz led off with a double to left center, and Ryan Billigan promptly delivered him home with a single to right center. When Neil Golden followed with a ground ball double down the third base line, Lou decided to make a pitching change, bringing in Georgie. But, although George got the two batters out on grounders to Joey, Billigan and then Golden crossed the plate on these successive plays, making the score 4-1.

In the top of the sixth, with one out, Nicky drew a walk off Ryan Billigan, on now in relief of Mitch Walters, and Joey singled to center, sending Nicky to third. Billy was up now, representing the tying run. On a 2-1 pitch, he sent a drive to deep left field. The ball seemed to have home run written all over it, but it was caught at the fence. Of very small consolation was the fact that Nicky was able to tag up and score after the catch. Ike was the Mets' last hope now, and he singled to left. Vinnie was the next batter, but his lack of speed hurt him, as his ground ball smash was knocked down in the hole at short by Steven Rourke, who had time to pick the ball up and throw Vinnie out. The game was over. Another tough game with the Reds, but nevertheless another loss for the Mets.

Game Two was scheduled for Saturday. Lou told his players not to get down. He explained to the boys that they'd played well, and indeed had come so close to evening up the score on Billy's long blast. "Come on, guys, we'll get them next game. Practice Friday afternoon, 5:30."

Chapter 26

Actually, Lou felt pretty good about the next game, as he drove home that night. He had the edge in pitching with Georgie over Ryan Billigan, and he was also of the opinion that his team was just hitting into hard luck, and things had a tendency to even out. But, he knew too that he was running out of time for proving it.

He decided to keep the mood of the practice light. His boys were obviously tense enough, so he wanted them to unwind and relax. A relaxed player, as long as he was focused on the game, always performed better, thought Lou.

So, on Friday, he permitted the clowning around by the usual cast of characters - Vinnie, Ike, and Chris, as long as they didn't start wrestling with each other. The last thing they needed was a senseless injury to somebody.

As practice ended, Lou, satisfied with what he'd witnessed, told the boys, "Get a good night's sleep, and I'll see you all tomorrow."

Chapter 27

It was a determined Met team that took the field on Saturday. After Georgie retired the Reds in order in the first inning, the Mets broke through for four big runs in the bottom half.

Georgie continued keeping the Reds at bay, and the Mets padded their lead, so that after four innings, the score was 8-1. Lou decided to gamble at this point, taking Georgie out, and bringing in Joey. Assuming the Mets would go on to win this game, he could still avail himself of Georgie's services for two innings tomorrow. Should Joey falter, Lou had the option of having Al pitch the final inning today.

Joey answered the call in the fifth inning, retiring the Reds in order. This was just what "the doctor ordered", felt Lou.

After the Mets were out in the bottom of the fifth, the Reds came up for their last at bats, trailing by seven.

But, things didn't go as smoothly this time. Two singles and a walk loaded the bases for Seth Kammawitz, who tattooed a ball over the fence for a grand slam homer. Just like that, 8-5 Mets. When the next batter walked, Lou had to bring in Al, after toying with the idea of calling on Ike, but deciding against it.

Al zipped through the next three batters, and the Mets had their victory. The team celebrated on the bench, but Lou was already thinking ahead to tomorrow, hoping he wouldn't need more than the Al/Georgie combo.

Chapter 28

That night, at the dinner table, Billy was talking about the game with his father.

"You know, son, I feel bad for Joey. I hope he doesn't get too down on himself. He's had his share of problems this year on the mound."

"Don't worry, Dad," replied Billy. "Joey's tough. In fact, much tougher than a lot of guys I know."

"Yourself included, Billy?"

"What do you mean, Dad?"

"Oh, nothing. Want to have a catch after supper?"

"Thanks, Dad, but I'm going over to Ronald's house. Next time, okay?"

"Yeah, sure. Next time."

Chapter 29

It was a beautiful Sunday Autumn afternoon, temperatures in the mid-70's, and the crowd on hand to watch the deciding semi-final game was larger than usual. Most of the Pirates were on hand, to see who'd they be playing. Even a lot of the Indians, Dodgers, and Angels were there.

The girls were out in full force, especially to be near Al.

"Hey, Al," screamed Pamela Goldsworthy, "who are you dedicating today's game to?"

"Myself, and my teammates, naturally," answered Al.

Lou was as tense as he'd ever been, but tried his best to mask it, remembering how beneficial Friday's "loose" practice had been for the Mets so far.

Paul Dodsworth poured over the scorebook to help himself ease the tension. He'd memorized each of the Mets-Reds games in his head. Now, he wanted to focus on what certain Reds hitters had done against both Al, who could go up to five innings today, and Georgie, who could go two.

The players on both teams looked determined during warm-ups. Bruce Plank, the Pirates star, yelled out to nobody in particular, "We can't wait to play the winner. The Pirates rule!"

Vinnie, who happened to be near Plank, decided to answer him back. "Hey Brucie, what are you basing that one on? Your 6-4 second half?"

"No, Pizza Face, our 9-1 first half."

"First half? That's ancient history, man. And watch who you're calling Pizza Face, buddy boy. Only my close friends can get away with that, and you're no friend of mine."

Al shouted out: "Hey, Vinnie, stop talking to him, and warm me up, will you?"

"Okay, Gusto. Put it right here."

After completion of warm-ups, Lou spoke to the team. "Okay, guys, let's try to get on top early. Let's play smart, and regardless of the score, keep your heads in the game. Al, you can go up to five innings today; Georgie, you can go two. Let's give it all we've got, alright?"

A collective "Let's go Mets" was shouted out in unison by the team, plus Lou and Dodsy, as they started moving about in the dugout.

Mitch Walters would pitch for the Reds today, and he could go six innings. Ryan Billigan, who had started yesterday but was ineffective, nevertheless was eligible for three frames as well.

The first inning went quickly for both teams, as all six batters were retired. But in the top of the second, consecutive singles by Ike, Vinnie, and Al loaded the bases with no one out. Georgie, up next, grounded weekly to short, forcing Al at second, but Ike scored the game's first run. Scotty was then hit by a pitch, re-loading the bases, and when Ronald walked on a 3-2 pitch, the Mets not only had a 2-0 lead, but a chance to break open the game with the top of the order up now.

Pete Billigan went out to the mound to calm Mitch Walters down. Whatever he said worked, as Nicky struck out and Joey flied out to left.

"I hope this doesn't come back to haunt us," Lou said to Dodsy as the Mets took the field. Lou was obviously thinking about the way many of the prior games with the Reds had turned out, amid Met would-be rallies often stymied.

He also knew how tough Mitch Walters could be, and that historically, he usually had one bad inning a game.

Al was looking real sharp today, and through the first three innings, had allowed only one base runner, Neil Golden, who had singled in the second.

But, at the same time, as his track record had indicated, Walters had settled down, and held the Mets scoreless in the third and fourth.

In the last of the fourth, Brian Sumner worked Al for a walk, and with Mitch Walters up, Al, perhaps trying too hard, uncorked a wild pitch, sending Sumner to second. With the count 3-1, Walters singled to center, Sumner holding up at third, respecting Billy's strong arm. Walters proceeded to steal second, and with Seth Kammawitz up, the Reds truly had a rally going. Al, pitching tough, got the dangerous Kammawitz to pop up to Joey. One out. Ryan Billigan was up. Al reared back, and ultimately fanned him. Two tough hitters, two big outs. Neil Golden up now, hoping to make it two for two against Al.

On a 2-1 pitch, Golden was able to ground it between short and third. Ike, ranging in the hole, managed to knock it down, but then made an ill-advised throw to first, although he really didn't have a shot at getting Golden. The hurried throw was wide of the bag, and got by Chris. Two runs scored, with Golden going to second. "Here we go again," murmured Lou in the dugout.

Al fanned the next batter, but now the game was tied, entering the fifth inning, Al's last on the mound no matter what.

Walters continued his fine performance, getting the Mets out 1-2-3, and Al returned the favor in the bottom half of the inning.

In the top of the sixth, Ike, leading off, singled to left. Vinnie popped up, but Al grounded a double just inside the third base bag, sending Ike to third. Pete Billigan had the Red's infield play half way, meaning they would be in position to either throw out Ike at the plate on a ground ball, or throw out the batter if Ike held at third. The Reds appeared to be geniuses when Georgie grounded to short. Ike momentarily held as the shortstop threw to first, but then decided to gamble by running home. The first baseman's throw to the plate, although a good one, was late, and the Mets were up 3-2. When he got to the bench, Ike looked at Lou and said, "I had to make up for my stupid play in the field, Mr. Skinner."

Scotty grounded out to second, and now, as the Mets took the field, they were three outs away from reaching the championship round.

It wouldn't be easy for Georgie, who, in relief of Al, had to face the heart of the Reds' lineup. Brian Sumner was up first, and he grounded to Joey, who threw him out. But Mitch Walters and Seth Kammawitz both singled, putting runners on first and second. Ryan Billigan then flied out to Scotty. The fly ball was deep enough so that both runners could tag up and advance one base, but now there were two outs.

Neil Golden, who had been a problem all day for the Mets, was up. With the count of 1-1, Golden did it again, grounding a single to center. Walters scored, and with Kammawitz lumbering behind him, Billy unleashed a magnificent throw to the plate, where Vinnie was planted. Vinnie didn't have to move at all to receive the perfect throw, and was able to put the tag on the hard-sliding Kammawitz to save the game and the season, at that point.

So, now it was on to extra innings. Walters could no longer pitch. Ryan Billigan came on. Unlike yesterday, however, the Mets could not immediately respond to Billigan, going out in order. Lou knew what that meant. Even if Georgie could hold the Reds scoreless, this would be his last inning on the hill.

Georgie made his final inning a good one, striking out the side in order. As the Mets came up for the eighth inning, Lou told Ike he would pitch in the bottom half. Joey had run into some tough luck against the Reds in previous games, and Lou felt there was no reason to tempt fate again.

Unfortunately, Ike was due up at bat this inning, cutting down his time to warm up. Would that be an issue, Lou asked himself?

Billy led off, and with the count 3-0, took a called first strike. The next pitch was right where Billy wanted it, and he parked it over the fence for a home run.

Ike then followed with a double, and came around to score on Al's single to right center. With the bench screaming for more, Georgie doubled Al to third, and after Scotty popped to the pitcher, Ronald grounded to second, Al scoring the third run of the inning. Nicky popped up to first, and Ike took the mound with a three run cushion.

Steven Rourke was set to lead off, and he singled to left. Brian Sumner lined a shot, but Joey made the catch, and there was one out. Mitch Walters was up. He stroked a double down the line, and Rourke scored easily.

Lou called time, and went to the mound. After talking to Ike, Joey, and Vinnie, they decided to "go against the book" and intentionally walk Seth Kammawitz, although that book says you are not supposed to put the potential winning run on base.

The strategy seemed to backfire, as Ryan Billigan, not exactly a slouch at the plate, singled to right, scoring Walters, and sending Kammawitz to third, with only one out. Now, Neil Golden was up, and so far he was 3-4 today. Ike was not pitching well, although at least he was throwing strikes.

On the first pitch, Billigan broke for second. Vinnie, not taking a chance on an errant throw, and with only one out, let him steal the base. The next pitch was lined over third, but foul by a small margin. With the count 2 and 2, Golden reached out and sent a drive to right centerfield. Both runners took off at the crack of the bat. Pete Billigan yelled at his runners to go back to their bases to tag up. Ryan Billigan never heard him, and was practically at third already, when Billy lunged and made a great catch. Joey yelled for the ball, Billy threw it to him, and Joey stepped on second base to complete the improbable double play. Kammazwitz, who had heard his coach and had retreated to third to tag up, was on his way to home plate after the catch and would have easily scored had Billigan played it more conservatively by staying closer to second base. Instead, the contest was abruptly over.

What an incredible end of a great game! The Reds, heart-broken, lined up to shake hands with the jubilant Mets.

When Lou got the team back in the dugout, he congratulated the boys, but then reminded them that their journey was far from over, for now the Pirates beckoned starting Thursday night.

As the team left, Lou thought about the performance of Billy today, and how it probably wouldn't have been required of his star to make all those plays in centerfield had Billy himself been on the mound in the first place. Although it was true that Lou had never seen Billy pitch, he was certain that Billy would excel there too, being the superb athlete he was, displaying an incredibly strong and accurate arm. Turning back to the reality of the situation at hand, Lou wondered if the team's luck would run out against the deeper pitching staff of the Pirates. Lou shook it off, and chuckled to himself that those extraordinary Billy plays in the outfield were sure fantastic to witness, and reminded himself to enjoy the victory, and worry about pitching matchups and depth later on.

"Great game, Billy," said Joey as the two were walking towards their parents' cars.

"Thanks, Joey, you were great, also," Billy replied. "I'll see you in school tomorrow."

"Okay, sure, Billy," Joey said, feeling strange. After all, they had been best friends for a few years, but now the relationship seemed strained, and very distant. As great as baseball was, and as exciting as today's victory had been, Joey nevertheless felt saddened as he got into the back seat of the car.

Chapter 30

Lou had made up his mind, even before next practice, to start Georgie in the first game of the Championship Series. Georgie and Al had both been great all year long, and there was little to choose from between them. Al had started the opener against the Reds, and now Lou felt he owed it to Georgie, as a way of "evening the score.".

There wasn't much to review or teach at practice. If the boys didn't know what to do by now, they never would, so Lou just let each kid get about twenty swings, and called it a night.

At home that evening, Dodsy once again "hit the books,", but not his school books. He was mulling over the stats, and the past contests versus the Pirates. He would give his analysis verbally to Lou at the game.

Chapter 31

George Porter and Bruce Plank, the first game starters, were warming up on their respective sidelines. The game soon began, and Plank, taking the mound for the home team Pirates, looked very confident. When he struck out Nicky and retired Joey on a popup, the Pirates hurler seemed to be laughing at the Mets. But Billy wiped the grin off Plank's face with a triple over the left fielder's head, and Ike delivered a clutch two out single, scoring Billy with the game's first run. Vinnie, remembering the verbal fight he'd gotten into with Plank last week, tried to take him deep, but his fly ball was caught, ending the top of the first.

Bruce Plank came up with two outs in the bottom of the first and no one on base. Lou had warned Vinnie not to say anything to Plank.

"Let sleeping dogs lie, Vinnie," Lou had told him.

"What's that mean exactly?"

"Well, it means, just don't say anything to arouse him, okay?"

As Plank took his stance at the plate, he glanced back at Vinnie, and said, "Think you've got us, huh? Think again, parmesan breath."

"Just play ball, Plank."

On a 2 and 1 pitch from Georgie, Plank unleashed a long fly to center, but Billy was able to haul it in for the third out.

It was all Vinnie could do to keep from saying anything to the Pirates star, but, recalling Lou's words, he instead directed his verbal outburst towards his own pitcher.

"Way to go, Georgie, way to be, man."

The Mets appeared confident and played with composure today, partly due to their already having been "through the wars" with the Reds, and emerging victorious. Eddie Howe, who had done little offensively for the Mets in this campaign, reached Plank for a single leading off the fourth, with the score still 1-0. After Marc Davidson popped up, Joey singled, and Billy doubled them both home. Billy had been something else in the playoffs. It seemed to Lou and the rest of the Mets that he was superhuman. Even his outs were hit very hard.

Ike grounded out, as the action resumed, with Billy going to third, but Vinnie came through with a hit, and it was now 4-0.

The Pirates chipped away for a run in the bottom of the fourth, but the Mets answered back with a run in the fifth, off Vic Spurgen, the second Pirates hurler.

Georgie breezed through his half of the fifth, and in the sixth, Lou decided to let Al pitch an inning. Al did give up a run, but it proved to be harmless, and the Mets were victorious, 5-2.

As the happy Mets listened to Lou's post game talk ("Great game, guys, but we still need one more"), Bruce Plank walked past their dugout, and said to them, "Don't get too excited, Mets, this was your last victory of the year."

"Let him talk, we'll do our thing on the field," Dodsy said as he noticed Vinnie and a few others getting ready to answer Plank.

"Boys, Paul is right," exclaimed Lou. "Let's concentrate on what still has to be done. Practice tomorrow at 5:30. OK?"

"OK," replied the Mets in unison.

Chapter 32

Joey could not sleep that night, and he already knew he would not sleep during the next two either. A lot of things were going through his mind.

First, of course, was the excitement connected with the anticipation of a championship. This was the closest he had personally ever been to one, and it was a great feeling. At the same time, however, he couldn't get out of his head the possibility that he would have to pitch again during the Championship Series. If he was so called upon, it would probably signify that the game was "on the line,", meaning a pressure situation, and Joey had been adequate at best on the hill this year. His mind was starting to play tricks on him, since every time he would think about pitching, it seemed that the Pirates were "teeing off" on him.

"Come on, Al, come on, Georgie," Joey muttered to himself. I'll do the fielding, and you guys do the pitching."

Chapter 33

Saturday morning was another gorgeous day, and with the game scheduled for a 1:00 start, the players were all at the field by 12:30.

There would be no tomorrow for the Pirates if they were to lose, and Bruce Plank, eligible to pitch three innings today, would start for them. For the Mets, Al Gustafson was being given the ball, and could pitch up to five innings, with George Porter eligible for one.

Plank was sharper today than he had been in Game one, and he enjoyed a 2-0 lead by the time he vacated the mound, after his three innings were over. With Vic Spurgen warming up for the Pirates, Plank stepped up to the plate against Al in the top of the fourth.

"Bet you're happy to see me finished, aren't you, Panzini?"

"Play ball, Plank. I'm not talking to you."

Play ball he did. He jumped on Al's first service and sent a rocket to left that easily cleared the fence for a home run. As he touched home plate, he murmured to Vinnie, "See you in Game Three, Jelly Belly."

It took great restraint on Vinnie's part to control himself. Luckily, Lou called time and went to the mound to settle Al down, and Vinnie joined them. Lou reminded Al that the score was still close, and that if they could keep the Pirates from doing any further scoring, the game would be up for grabs.

Al responded, getting slugger Bill Washington on a comebacker to the mound, and Jason Satriano on a popup. Lenny Fielder then struck out, and the Mets were up, looking for a rally.

Plank had retired nine of the ten Mets he'd faced, but now Vic Spurgen had to contend with Joey, Billy and Ike in the bottom of the fourth.

Joey hit it hard, but right at Plank, now playing shortstop. Still, even with the out, the Mets sensed something good would happen, and that they'd be able to get to Spurgen. They were right.

Billy, again coming through, doubled down the left field line, and Ike walked. Vinnie was up, and he never wanted to come up with a hit more than now. His body responded to his mind, as he doubled over the right fielder's head, scoring both runners. It was now a 3-2 game. Vinnie danced off second base, as Spurgen tried to get a hold of himself and pitch to Al.

"Hey, Brucie baby, I'm scoring also and I won't be the last run this inning, either. The only way you'll see me tomorrow is if I invite you over to look at my trophy." Vinnie knew he probably shouldn't have said anything, but he couldn't help himself any longer.

"Shut up, fat boy," replied Bruce.

Vinnie's prophecy about the fourth inning proved to be semi-true, for on a wild pitch he went to third, where he scored on a ground ball out to second by Al, tying the game. But Georgie then popped up for out number three.

The score stayed deadlocked at three apiece through the fifth inning, and entering the sixth inning, Georgie took the mound for the Mets. Now, with one out, Vic Spurgen was up. He could really help himself here with the lumber.

Georgie didn't want to walk him, with Plank and Washington to follow. Perhaps he grooved a pitch too much, for Spurgen took him deep for a double over Billy's head. At that point, Lou called time and visited the mound.

"Georgie, you can only go one inning today. Don't hold anything back."

Georgie nodded, and set himself up to pitch to Bruce Plank.

On a 2 and 2 pitch, Georgie hurled a high, hard fastball, and Plank foul tipped it, but right into Vinnie's mitt for a strikeout.

"Thanks for the tip, Brucie," Vinnie yelled out.

Two outs now, Bill Washington up. He walked. Next was Jason Satriano, but he never got to swing the bat. On the first pitch, a ball low in the dirt, Vic Spurgen took off for third, and Vinnie gunned him down with a perfect strike to Ike.

Vinnie was having a great game, and now he was being mobbed by his teammates on the bench. At the same time, Lou was contemplating what to do about a pitcher for the next inning, should there be one, as Georgie could not go out there again, under league rules.

Lou decided to have Joey warm up. Of course, if the Mets could push a run across the plate in the bottom of the sixth, the game (and the season) would be over.

Scotty would lead off against Vic Spurgen who, as reminded by his manager Mike Plank, was also in his last inning of pitching. Spurgen was throwing hard now, and he struck Scotty out. Ronald was now up, but all he could do was to popup weakly to the pitcher's mound. Nick tried to bunt his way on, but he couldn't place it where he wanted to, and Spurgen easily threw him out.

Oh well, here we go again, muttered Joey to himself, as he trotted out to the mound and began his warmup tosses from the rubber.

Lou ordinarily would remind his pitcher in this spot that he was facing the lower part of the opposition's batting order, but he figured that Joey, a real student of the game, already knew that, plus Lou didn't want Joey letting up, for the Pirates had tough hitters throughout their entire lineup.

Four batters later, and Joey, Lou, and the rest of the Mets saw again just how potent the Pirates squad could be. Jason Satriano led off the seventh with a single, and after Lenny Fielder flied out to left, John Simon and Don Hearn, batters eight and nine, both singled, Satriano scoring.

They were hitting Joey hard, and with the top of the Pirate order to contend with, Lou brought in Ike to relieve Joey.

Ike, unfortunately, wasn't much better, as he walked Eric Stein to load the bases. Freddy Pointer, up for the Pirates, singled in one run, and another crossed the plate when Scotty's throw back to the infield was an errant one.

With runners on second and third, a blowout looked realistic, especially since the Pirates had Spurgen up, with Plank and Washington to follow.

But Spurgen was a little too anxious, and he struck out on a bad pitch, for out number two. Ike, pitching carefully to Plank, walked him, re-loading the bases. Bill Washington stood in, and he made a strong bid for a grand slam, flying deep to center, where Billy made the catch for the third out.

Although most observers agreed it could have been worse, the Mets were still down by three runs in the bottom of the seventh. Joey led off, and the first pitch from Lenny Fileder, now in relief for the Pirates, hit him in the back. Joey was alright, as he shook it off and trotted to first.

Billy was next, and for one of the very few times in a clutch situation Lou could remember, his star player did not come through, flying out to center. Ike was now up, and he singled to left. Vinnie, on fire all day, also singled. With the Mets' bench, as well as their families and friends going crazy, Al stepped up to the plate, representing the winning run. On a 2 and 1 pitch, he hit a hard ground ball in the hole between where the new shortstop Eric Stein was, and the second base bag. But, as the ball appeared to be on its way into center field, it took one of those "charity hops" that a fielder loves, which not only slowed the ball down, but also bounced perfectly for Stein, whose throw to first just nipped Al for the second out. One run did come in, and now the tying run was in scoring position at second, with Georgie up.

Fielder worked the count to one ball and two strikes, and when the next pitch, in a perfect spot on the outside corner of the plate, was called a strike by the umpire, the game was suddenly over. The Pirates had won it, 6-4, setting up tomorrow's contest that would decide everything. Lou's game plan, in talking to his players on the bench now, was to make sure they didn't feel incapable of winning a close game against a good team.

"Boys," Lou started, "it's been a long season, and it's been a great one. You guys have played the top teams, which of course are the Pirates and the Reds, and you've stood toe to toe with them all the time. You've won some big games. Remember the first half playoff game against the Reds? We came out smoking that day, and that was on the heels of having lost a heartbreaker to them. What about our 3-2 win over the Pirates in the first half? And, let's not forget the deciding game in the semifinals against the Reds. Guys, we're a tough team, certainly as tough as the Pirates, and we should feel good about our chances Sunday. Let's get a good night's rest, and I'll see you all tomorrow."

On the way home, Lou again was contemplating the pitching matchups for tomorrow. The Pirates could once more utilize Plank and Spurgen for up to three innings each, with Fielder available for up to five innings. On the other side, Georgie could go five, and Al one. Certainly, Pirate manager Mike Plank had more options to exercise. Boy, what I'd give to have his staff, thought Lou, but that thought was quickly replaced by another one: I've got a great bunch of kids, and I wouldn't trade them for anyone. We'll beat them with what we've got, somehow.

Chapter 34

Melvin Jeffries waited until dinner that night to say what he'd been meaning to ask Billy for quite some time.

"You know, son, you and Joey don't seem to be as close as you used to be. Just my imagination, or am I right?"

"We're still good friends, Dad," answered Billy.

"Good friends perhaps, very close, no," observed Billy's father. "How do you feel about it?"

"Dad, I don't feel good about it at all. As a matter of fact, it's been eating away at me. You see, Joey's been having a tough time this year, pitching in some tough situations and usually not coming through too well. He doesn't say much about it, but I know, deep down, he blames me."

"Blames you?" chimed in Claire Jeffries. "But why?"

"Because, Mom, he thinks I should be pitching instead of him, that's why."

"Yes, well, why won't you son?" asked his father.

With tears in his eyes, Billy slowly began telling his parents the story of how, at age nine, he'd been pitching and had proceeded to hit three consecutive batters, each one worse than before, the last child crying as he was carried off the field. Billy remembered like it was only yesterday how badly he felt, and how scared he was to continue pitching. Now, finally, he'd confided in someone, and he felt a tremendous burden being lifted from his shoulders.

"Son, I remember that day as well," said Mr. Jeffries, "but I had no idea you still felt that way."

"Why do you think I haven't pitched since then?"

"I guess I never thought about it," answered his father. "But, Billy, think about your relationship with Joey. You guys used to be inseparable."

"I do, Dad, it really bothers me, but I just can't help it."

"Maybe," said his mother, "you should tell Joey the entire story. I'm sure he'd understand."

"Maybe someday, but I can't tell him or anyone else right now. Excuse me, I'm going to my room." With that, Billy quickly ran up the steps to his bedroom, still tormented by the past.

Chapter 35

Paul Dodsworth was speaking to Joey Harrison on the phone that night. He knew his friend was upset about having been the losing pitcher today, and was now trying to cheer him up.

"Joey, I have this feeling, I really do, that you're going to get the winning hit tomorrow. My pal, the hero."

"Thanks, Dodsy. I hope you're right," uttered an uncertain Joey Harrison.

Al Gustafson told his mother that if any of the girls called to speak to him, she was to tell them that he wasn't home.

"But, Al," said his mother, "I hate to see you so tensed up. It's only a game."

"Mom, those annoying girls make me more tense than anything else."

Ike Eichorn was on the phone with Georgie Porter.

"Georgie, I'm a little nervous about tomorrow. What about you?"

Georgie said to Ike: "Yeah, maybe a little, but I'll be okay once I warm up. It's the waiting around that's rough."

The way Georgie and Ike felt pretty much summed up the way each of the participants on both teams were approaching the final game: Nervous, anxious, a fear of doing something bad to lose the game, a dream of being the hero.

None of them would get much sleep tonight.

Chapter 36

Lou tried to sleep, but found he couldn't, and instead, his thoughts drifted back to the days when he, himself, played Little League. A few of the teams he had been a member of during his childhood had been to the playoffs, and he had little trouble remembering either the circumstances or the participants. It's funny, thought Lou, I can't recall what I did last month, but yet I can recreate with historical accuracy what transpired all those years ago.

One series of events stuck out in his mind. It was when Lou was fourteen years old, during the playoffs that year. Lou's team had been in first place all season long, due in no small part to having the league's most dominant player, Nat Andrews. Nat was a hard-throwing, right handed pitcher, who reminded people of a young Bob Gibson. Nat was undefeated all year, and the team was easing its way towards a championship. But, as the season ran down, the team's fine catcher, Joel Burger, found out he had made his school's football team and his father, fearing Joel would be exhausted, forbid him to play both sports simultaneously, and so Joel was coerced into giving up baseball. Unfortunately, the team had only one other catcher, and that was Nat Andrews. Since it is physically impossible to both pitch and catch at the same time, the team was forced to use a succession of marginal pitchers towards the end of the regular season, and lost their last three games, stumbling into the playoffs. You see, when Lou was a kid, games were only once a week. Therefore, until the incident with Joel Burger, Nat had been able to pitch every game. The squad, at one time sporting an 11-0 record, finished at 11-3.

The prospects of winning the playoffs looked dim, for Lou's club was a relatively weak hitting one. A typical score when Nat pitched was 2-0. Scoring two runs now, with either Denny McGlintz or Vic Ebbets pitching instead of Nat would not cut it.

Fifteen minutes before game time of the semi-finals (a one-game elimination scenario, as would be the finals), Lou had an idea.

"Guys, I'll catch," yelled Lou to his teammates, who were warming up.

"Lou, have you ever caught before?" questioned center fielder Horace Dennington.

"No, but at least this way Nat gets to pitch. Let's face it, it's our only chance to win."

"Yeah, but Lou," shouted Vic Ebbets, "you're left handed, and there's no such thing as a lefty catcher's mitt. You use your fielder's glove, and he'll break your hand right off."

At that point, Lou picked up the catcher's mitt and said, "No problem. I'll just wear it backwards on my catching hand"

Lou proceeded to take warm-up tosses from Nat, the mitt indeed on the opposite hand. As the game started, it took several of his teammates to dress him in the catcher's gear of mask, chest protector, and shin guards, things he'd never worn before in his life. For a protective cup, he used his baseball cap, and hoped that the brim of the cap would be good enough.

In any event, by the fifth inning, the team and Lou were surviving, out in front 5-0, and Lou kept mercifully (for him) signaling for the curve ball. But Nat kept shaking him off, feeling he couldn't control his curve that day. Lou's hand was killing him, but he was still feeling good about the decision he'd made.

When the game had ended, the team, playing loosey goosey with their star on the mound, broke out of a season long batting slump and hit/scored more

93

than they had in the last several games combined, and were victorious 10-0. Lou became the talk of the neighborhood.

Lou and his father looked all over town for a lefty catcher's mitt, but were unsuccessful. Lou finally had to settle for adding a new piece of "equipment" to his arsenal, a sponge to place inside the catcher's mitt, in an attempt to cushion the force of Nat's blistering fastball.

Lou was enjoying his week of being in the spotlight. After all, their squad all year had, up until now, been kind of one-dimensional.

The team they'd be playing for the title was a tough one, led by lefty pitcher Tommy Haynes, but Lou's team was supremely confident with Nat on the mound. Lou, feeling relaxed at the plate, went two for two, plus a walk and a sacrifice bunt. He also threw out two base runners who'd attempted to steal that day, and his club won the championship 4-1. Lou was a real hero, and for him, it was like being on Cloud 9.

As Lou lay in bed, a smile came to his face. Twenty-one years later, he now wondered what had become of his old teammates, as well as the righty catcher's mitt he had successfully worn on the "wrong" hand. That glove's probably at Cooperstown, mused Lou as he turned over.

Lou was also contemplating what kind of drama would unfold tomorrow in the championship game against the Pirates. If the game were to take its normal course, it figured to be close, with either squad capable of winning. But, would it actually follow form, or would something unexpected occur?

By tomorrow afternoon, Lou and the rest of Springtown would know.

Chapter 37

Sunday morning finally rolled around, and it looked to be another fantastic day outside. Joey, up early, opened the front door to pick up the newspaper that had been delivered. Protesting but to no avail that he wasn't hungry, his mother prepared breakfast.

"Joey, you can't play ball on an empty stomach," Jeannie Harrison firmly stated.

"Okay, Mom, but not too much," Joey said, resigned to the fact that he could not totally overrule her.

Joey had his face buried in the sports section while he was eating, and hardly noticed his father entering the kitchen.

"Morning," said Dan Harrison.

"Good morning, honey," replied his wife. Joey continued reading the paper.

"What's the matter, are you deaf, Joey?" questioned his father.

"What? Oh, sorry, Dad. I didn't hear you. Did you say something?"

"Never mind. What time's the game?"

"One o'clock," answered Jeannie. "We have to be there by 12:30."

"Okay, but if we left it up to Joey, we'd be leaving now, right son?"

"Er, good morning, Dad," spoke Joey, several beats behind his parents this morning.

"Joey, eat your breakfast." As Dan motioned to his wife to follow him into the next room, he turned to her and said, "You know, Jeannie, I wish he'd study his subjects in school as doggedly as he reads the sports section of the paper. But I guess I'll leave him alone today. Let him have his moment in the sun, as they say."

"I just hope that, even if they lose, Joey doesn't have a bad game, doing something directly responsible for the loss. He'll be tough to live with after that," commented Jeannie.

"It's all a part of growing up, honey. Believe me, I'd rather see the Mets win today. But if they don't, he'll survive it somehow."

"I know, Dan. It's just that Joey seems to have felt personally responsible for some of the losses, and each time it was when he was pitching. I hope he doesn't have to pitch today."

"Jeannie, to tell you the truth, I've been thinking the same thing. You know, I ran into Lou Skinner last night at the Convenience Store. We talked about how great the season has been overall. Then we spoke about Joey. He told me that Joey is one of the most mature boys he's ever met for his age, and that he's been a real pleasure to coach. I told him that Joey's maturity would surely be tested if he were to pitch in the last game and fail. You know what Lou said then? He said just what I told you a few minutes ago, that it was part of growing up, that it would be painful for a while, but Joey would get over it eventually. Plus, his friends on the Mets love Joey. They would never get on his case, and if anything, they would share in the blame should they lose."

Jeannie replied, "That was nice of Lou to say about our son. Why don't you tell Joey?"

"I will, but after the game, win or lose. Right now, Joey seems so totally focused on baseball, and while he may be staring at professional box scores in the paper, he's also day-dreaming, I'm sure, about this afternoon."

"So, I guess you feel it would lose its effect at this moment. I can't argue with that, Dan. Let me ask you a question. Were you as good a player at Joey's age?"

"There are five ways you measure a ballplayer, Jeannie. Hitting, hitting with power, fielding, running, and throwing. Joey's got the thirteen year old version of your husband beat in all five categories. Plus, he's got the ability to perform under pressure. Better than I could, that's for sure. He's so smooth at short and looks confident at the plate, no matter who the opposition is. He may not be the world's greatest pitcher, but he's a heck of a ballplayer. Anyway, we'd better get dressed. I've got a sneaky suspicion our son wants to get there early."

Chapter 38

The parking lot was jam-packed today. This was an event that brought out not only the parents of the players, but grandparents, friends, and other players in the league as well, such as Ryan Billigan, Mitch Walters, and Seth Kammawitz of the Reds, and Wally Seedman of the Indians. Actually, all of the Reds would be on hand today to receive their second-half first place trophies. There would also be trophies for the Pirates, for winning the first half. Lastly, there would be trophies for the winners of today's contest, and the runner-up awards for today's losers.

As the league officials arrived and transported the four sets of trophies from their cars to the area of the playing field, all eyes were riveted in that direction. The players on both the Pirates and the Mets stopped warming up for a moment, as they got caught up in the pageantry and regality of what the award ceremony would mean later on.

Dan Harrison, seated in the bleachers, turned to his wife, and said, "You know, Jeannie, the ways the boys stopped dead in their tracks just now reminds me of the time I was at a trade show in Chicago. Both our booth and the one opposite my company's were filled with people. There was the usual amount of chatting and movement you'd expect on a show's first day. Just then, Joe DiMaggio, who was there at the show as a spokesperson for another company, walked down our aisle. At that moment, everybody stopped what they were doing and just watched this great man walk by. Not a word was spoken by anyone, and it was as though time was frozen because, I'm telling you, we were all like mannequins then. I'll never forget that scene. I don't know, the way the kids were staring at the trophies just reminded me of that."

Back on the field, Vinnie shouted out, "Man, oh man, look at those big trophies, Dodsy."

"Yeah, they're awesome," Dodsy replied.

On the other side of the field, a supremely confident Bruce Plank shouted out to the league officials, "I hope those big suckers have the name Pirates on them, because that's who's getting them."

"Bruce," directed Mike Plank, "never mind that kind of talk now. Let's win the game first, alright?"

"Yeah, alright, Dad."

Lou Skinner's mind was racing back and forth right about now. If Georgie was on his game, the Mets would have an edge on the mound, since Bruce Plank could only pitch three innings today, and Vic Spurgen had been hittable so far. That was a plus. On the other hand, should Georgie falter, or should the game go into extra innings again, Lou's bullen after Al (who could only go one inning) was no match for that of the Pirates. That was a minus. Lou kept glancing down the right field foul line, where Georgie was warming up. He knew it was tough to gauge a pitcher by warm-ups. Often, you could be great before the game, but stink up the place once the contest unfolded. The opposite also could hold true. Then again, you could be sharp both before and during the game. Yes, impossible to gauge, thought Lou.

At this point, it was the Mets' turn to take pregame fielding practice. As Lou fungoed out grounders to the infield, and fly balls to the outfield, it was hard to get a reading on the team's mental state. They didn't seem nervous, nor did they appear loose or overconfident. More business-like than anything else.

As he led the team back to the dugout, Lou decided to keep the speech short and sweet. No need to remind them about the game's importance. Rather, after reviewing the signs (take, bunt, swing away, steal), he elected to focus on the opposition.

"Boys, we've played the Pirates enough to know their tendencies very well. Keep in mind, they are very aggressive at the plate. They'll swing on 2 and 0 or 3 and 1 counts. In fact, we've seen Plank and Spurgen swing away on 3 and 0. Ike and Ronald, watch for Stein to bunt. He's clever. Sometimes he'll wait until the count is something like 2 and 1 before laying one down."

Vinnie interjected, "Freddy Pointer bunts a lot, also."

"That's right, Vinnie, good point. Also, infielders, because of the weather this last week, the grass is higher than normal. So, you guys are going to have to really charge the ball today. Outfielders, don't forget to back each other up, okay? That's all I've got to say, except for one thing. No matter what the score is, play real hard and keep your heads in the game. Neither team is out of it until the last out has been made. Dodsy, you have anything to add?"

Dodsy, ever the keen student of the game, came up with the following: "Yeah, two things. When they try to steal a base, it's almost always on the first pitch. Also, all their batters after Washington have not been able to pull Georgie or Al all year. So, when righties hitting sixth, seventh, eighth, or ninth are up, our first and second basemen and right fielder should be ready, and vice versa for the lefties."

"Thanks, Dodsy," said Lou. "Now, boys, let's go get 'em, alright?"

A collective "alright" boomed from the mouths of the Mets. Then, as Dodsy read the starting lineup, Lou walked towards home plate, converging with Mike Plank who was coming from his dugout, as they met with the umpires to discuss the ground rules.

"Let's have a good game, fellas," stated the home plate ump in conclusion, as Mike and Lou shook hands.

Before undoubtedly the largest crowd in Springtown's history, the game was finally ready to begin. The Mets against the Pirates, for all the marbles.

As his Pirates teammates ran onto the field, Bruck Plank strode to the mound with his usual confident swagger. For added effect, as Plank fired his warm-ups, catcher Jason Satriano shook his glove hand upon each reception, as if to signify that Plank was throwing so hard, it was hurting him.

Mets' leadoff batter Nicky Plugman tried to get things started by laying down a bunt, but his attempt went foul. Eventually, Nicky grounded to short-stop Eric Stein, who calmly threw to Bill Washington for the first out of this championship game.

Joey Harrison stepped in, determined to get things started. Joey hit the ball decently, but it was too high in the air, and it became an easy catch for center fielder John Simon. Two out, and nobody on, but now Billy Jeffries was up. Plank pitched carefully to Billy, too carefully in fact, and Billy walked. Now, Ike Eichorn stepped in, and on the first pitch, Satriano had trouble coming up with it, and Billy easily trotted to second. Ike worked the count to 3 and 1, but then he seemed over-anxious, swinging at what probably would have been ball four, and he lifted a pop-up to second that Freddy Pointer, back-peddling, gathered in for out number three.

Georgie Porter marched out to the mound to face the Pirates in the bottom of the first. Eric Stein, the Pirate leadoff batter, had to fight off a tough inside pitch with two strikes on him, and he hit a weak popup to the mound area that Georgie corraled. Next was John Simon, and his ground ball to short was charged perfectly by Joey, who completed the play for out number two. Vic Spurgen stepped in, and drilled Georgie's first pitch cleanly into center field for a base hit. That brought Bruce Plank up to the plate. Plank worked the count to 2 and 2, and as the next pitch came in, he took it, and was very surprised to hear the umpire bellow out "Strike Three." Plank had to control himself against any outburst which could get him thrown out of the game, so he directed his anger at Georgie.

"You got me this time, Porter; my turn, next time," he yelled.

Plank was seething on the mound now, and after walking Vinnie to start the second inning, he reared back and in turn struck out Al and Georgie on blazing fastballs, before completing the half inning by getting Scotty on a weak grounder to second base.

In the bottom of the second, the tough Bill Washington lined a shot just inside the third base foul line, and hustled into second just ahead of Gusto's throw, for a leadoff double. When Jason Satriano grounded to second, Nicky fumbled it, but was able to recover and throw him out, with Washington taking third. Now Lenny Fielder was up, and he grounded sharply in the hole between first and second. Ronald Carson made a fine stop, and flipped underhanded to Georgie, covering the bag for the out. It was a great play, but Washington scored, and the Pirates were on the board first. Georgie, composing himself, struck out Freddy Pointer.

The Pirates had jumped out to a 1-0 lead. Now, to the top of the third, and Chris Conley pinch-hitting for Ronald Carson. This was a little earlier than normal for such a change, but Lou's reasoning was this: All players in uniform, whether starters or subs, had to play the equivalent of six consecutive outs in the field at a minimum, and bat at least once. Under Little League rules, players taken out could re-enter later in the same game. So, Lou figured, he could exercise his option now and bring back the speedy Ronald as early as the fifth inning.

In any event, the strategy looked good right away, as Chris blooped a ball that had "eyes", and it fell to the ground between the second baseman and the right fielder of the Pirates for a base hit. Donnie Bowman was up now, to pinch hit for Nicky. Again, the bench did its job. Even though Mike Plank yelled out to his troops to watch for the bunt, the Pirates had only one play on the beauty

Donnie laid down, Jason Satriano just nipping him at first for the out. Chris was now in scoring position at second, with only one out. Now it was Joey's turn, and he made the most of it, grounding a single up the middle. Joey, always the thinking man's player, took a real wide turn at first, making like he had visions of going to second. This caused first baseman Bill Washington, who was standing on the mound, to cut off the throw from John Simon. Chris scored easily, and Joey scampered back to first, beating the throw from Washington to the covering Freddy Pointer.

This was one of those plays you had to marvel at, in that the execution on the part of both of the baserunners was flawless, something you might not expect from kids. However, it was obvious that these were not ordinary kids but rather superb athletes who were well drilled. Even the Pirates played it correctly by hitting the cutoff man. This was the sort of action that signified a championship game.

In the meantime, the Mets bench was alive.

"Way to go, Joey," shouted Dodsy.

"Way to be, Chris. That's getting it going," beamed a happy Lou.

Mike Plank called time and paid his son a visit on the mound, reminding him that this was his last inning of pitching, and that he was to throw nothing but heat to Jeffries and Eichorn here. Bruce nodded in understanding, took a deep breath, and prepared himself for the task at hand.

Billy, stepping in, was as tough a batter as anyone would want to face, but this time Plank got the better of him, as he induced Billy to ground to second for a force out. When Ike followed with a fly out to left, Mike Plank heaved a momentary sigh of relief.

Georgie was facing a pinch hitter, Larry Nelson, in the bottom of the third. Georgie got him on a comebacker to the mound. But Eric Stein, on a

2 and 1 count, reached Georgie for a base hit, and with John Simon up, Stein took second on a wild pitch. Georgie then made a good pitch, getting Simon to ground out to first, Stein reaching third. Vic Spurgen walked on a 3 and 1 count, and stole second on the first pitch to Bruce Plank. Lou was afraid to put Plank on via an intentional pass now, with Bill Washington on deck.

Georgie pitched tough to Plank, and induced the fine cleanup hitter to ground it to third. But the usually sure handed Ike couldn't come up with the ball cleanly, and all hands were safe, Stein scoring, giving the Pirates the lead back.

Georgie didn't let it get to him, however, and retired Washington on a grounder to Joey.

Half the contest had elapsed, and the Pirates were winning. Obviously it was still anybody's game. How would it end? Which team would emerge victorious?

Vic Spurgen took his warm-up throws at the top of the fourth, and scheduled up for the Mets were Vinnie, Gusto, and Georgie. Vinnie grounded to short, where Bruce Plank was, and Plank threw him out easily. Davey Filstein was sent up to hit for Al now, so Gusto could be back in the game in the sixth inning, to pitch. Davey, a fine fielder but somewhat deficient with the stick, struck out. Georgie then popped up to Bill Washington. Three up, three down, and rather easily.

Lou had to be concerned. The Mets had handled Spurgen better in the two previous encounters. Spurgen looked sharp today. Georgie had to hold the Pirates down now.

Jason Satriano was to lead off, and Mike Plank told his team to get more.

"The final score of this game won't be 2-1, guys. Let's increase the lead."

Satriano looped a ball into short left field and, running hard, could have possibly gotten as far as second base, but instead he and the rest of the Pirates could only watch in amazement at the sensational play Joey made. The excellent shortstop ran with his back to home plate, diagonally towards the foul line, caught the ball, and held onto it as he fell and rolled over. Truly, a remarkable play for a thirteen year old.

Georgie uncharacteristically ran over to Joey. "Gimme five, Joey. Alright! Great play."

"Thanks, Georgie," replied Joey, shyly.

On the bench, Dodsy, Lou and the others were whooping it up. Dodsy especially felt good for his friend, who was such a steady ballplayer, he was often taken for granted.

"That's one for the highlight film, Joey," Dodsy yelled out.

Mike Plank tried to get his team re-focused on the game, but it seemed as though the momentum was clearly with Georgie and his squad now. Stu Roberts, a pinch hitter, struck out on three pitches. Freddy Pointer was next, and he didn't fare any better, fanning on a 1 and 2 hard one to end the inning.

As everybody on the Mets poured over to Joey on the bench, the shortstop reminded them, "Guys, we're still losing this game. We've got a job to do now."

"Joey's right," said Vinnie. "Let's go get 'em."

This might, thought Lou, be easier said than done, as Eddie Howe went down on strikes for the first out in the top of the fifth. But Ronald, back in the game, walked.

"That's getting it started," shouted Dodsy, who was amazed at the number of times Ronald had drawn a base on balls this year. He had led the team in that department last year, and was doing it again, despite rarely playing the entire six innings of a game.

Nicky, up now with one out, grounded in the hole between short and third. Eric Stein, at third, knocked the ball down, picked it up, and threw to second in an attempt for a force play, but the speedy Ronald beat the throw. Two runners on, one out, and Joey up.

"C'mon, Joey," Lou shouted.

Joey was up in a big spot, but for some reason he wasn't tense at all. He couldn't wait to do battle with Vic Spurgen. Joey's brilliant fielding play just may have gotten him into a loose but yet combative frame of mind.

Joey wasn't especially known for his power hitting, but this time he rocketed a ball over Stu Roberts' head in left. Both runners scored, and Joey stood on second base with a double, slapping his hands together in a rare (for him) show of emotion, as the Met bench and their supporters in the stands were going nuts.

Lou yelled out to Joey that there was only one out. Even as "tuned in" a player as Joey was, he could lose sight of the game situation in a moment like this. Joey nodded back to Lou, as if to say, "Gotcha."

Billy was up now with a chance to really do some damage. Spurgen was pitching carefully to the Mets' star hitter, and on a 2 and 1 count, Billy reached for an outside pitch, and smashed a one-hopper that Bill Washington was able to glove, and retire Billy by stepping on the first base bag. Joey moved over to third, but now there were two outs.

Ike stepped in, and what followed was a further display of the breaks of the game. Whereas Billy couldn't have hit the ball any harder but yet had nothing to show for it, Ike, taking a full cut, was only able to muster a dribbler down the third base line that he beat out for an infield hit, Joey scoring to give the Mets a 4-2 advantage.

Vinnie then tried to give his side more, but he flied out to right to retire the Mets.

It was an exciting moment for the Mets, but Lou knew the game was far from being over.

With the Pirates' supporters cheering their team on, Don Hearn drew a leadoff walk, something obviously Lou didn't want to see. He called time, and went out to talk to Georgie.

"Georgie, a couple of things. First of all, these guys are all hitters. I doubt if they'll be taking a strike. Unless the count is 3 and 0, don't lay anything in. Also, remember, this is your last inning of pitching. Keep bringing it, OK?"

Georgie nodded his head in assent, and prepared himself for Eric Stein. Lou's assessment proved to be right, as Stein, first-ball swinging, popped up to Nicky. John Simon up now, worked the count to 3 and 1, but Georgie reminded himself not to groove the next pitch, and he induced the Pirates center fielder to hit a grounder to Ronald, who beat Simon to the bag, Hearn taking second.

Vic Spurgen was up in a real pressure situation, and he came through with a big hit, singling to left center, Hearn scoring. Now it was a 4-3 game.

Bruce Plank strode up to the plate, representing the go-ahead run. I can't let Harrison be the hero of the game, felt Plank as he took his stance.

Here was a classic confrontation: A great pitcher facing a great hitter. Who would win out?

Plank did, shooting a vicious two-hopper to the fence in left center, scoring Vic Spurgen all the way from first. Billy did all he could just to keep Plank at second by getting the ball in quickly and accurately. Bruce Plank had done it again. Brand new ballgame at four runs apiece, and the strong bat of Bill Washington loomed on the horizon.

Lou again called time, and went to the mound a second time (Three visits to the mound in one inning necessitated a pitching change in this league, so Lou had this trip to spare).

"Georgie, do you want to pitch to Washington, or walk him and pitch to Satriano?"

Georgie was remarkably poised for someone who has just seen his lead vanish in this most important of games.

In a tone more business-like than sorrowful, Georgie answered, "I'll pitch to Satriano, coach."

"Okay, let's do it."

Washington was thus intentionally passed, and as Satriano stepped in, Georgie became so attentive to the task at hand, he could barely hear Bruce Plank, standing at second base, shouting, "You're finished now, Porter. C'mon, Jason. Put them away."

Georgie looked into Vinnie's mitt, and threw a bullet that Satriano

took at the knees for strike one. The next pitch was fouled back. Strike two.

With the collective eyes of everyone there intently following the action, Georgie reared back and fired a low, hard one that may have been a little low, but Satriano could take no chances. He swung, and he missed. The side was out. Lou breathed a sigh of relief, but the reality of the situation was that the game was indeed tied, with one inning to go.

Gusto was set to lead off the sixth. He had warmed up on the sidelines last inning, and he felt ready to go. "I've got to get things started, so I can take the mound with a lead," he said to Dodsy, as he left the dugout.

"You can do it Al," replied Dodsy.

Gusto completely foiled the Pirates, who didn't expect him to bunt. But bunt he did, down the first base line, and now there was going to be a real race to the bag, as Vic Spurgen pounced off the mound, picked up the ball and ran with it. Bill Washington was in too close, as he had reacted to the bunt by charging it, and he was in no position to scamper back to first. Who would get to the bag first, Spurgen or Gusto?

It was Gusto, but as he tried to overstride to beat out Spurgen, he hit the front end of the bag in a funny way, and toppled over. Time was called, and Lou ran over to his fallen player. Gusto seemed to be in real pain. It appeared as though he had really twisted his ankle, and maybe it was even broken. Lou called out for an ice pack.

"Coach, it's killing me," moaned Al, "but I've gotta be in there."

"Sorry, Al, but there is no way you can play any more today. Come on, I'll help you to the bench."

As Davey Filstein went into to run for Al, Lou yelled out, "Joey, you'd better warm up. You're pitching this next inning."

Nothing could have been worse, Joey felt, than to have heard those words from Lou. Joey was a confident ballplayer, but he knew he had deficiencies in pitching, especially against a robust lineup like the Pirates.

At that moment, something really unpredictable occurred. Billy moved over on the bench so he was next to Joey, put his arm around his friend, and after looking back towards the stands at his parents, said, "You won't have to go out there, Joey. I'll pitch."

"That's okay, Billy. I'll do it," answered Joey.

"No, Joey. This is something I've got to do for myself as well as for you."

Lou had overheard this conversation, and moved over to Billy. "Are you sure, Billy?"

"Yeah, I'm sure, coach."

"Okay, go ahead and warm up."

Joey looked over at his long time friend, and with both admiration and a sigh of relief, echoed, "Go get 'em, Billy."

As all of this was taking place, Georgie stepped into the batter's box, and with real determination, stroked a single over second base, Davey stopping at second. Scotty Edwards, attempting a sacrifice bunt, popped it in the air, where Vic Spurgen called for and caught it for out number one. Ronald Carson, on a 2-2 pitch, was called out on strikes. But Nicky worked out a walk, and that brought up Joey with the bases loaded and two outs.

This had been Joey's day so far, both in the field and at the plate, but that was history. There could be no resting on past laurels.

Maybe it was the idea of Billy pitching instead of him, or perhaps it was the supreme confidence Joey now had, based on his performance today, but again Joey felt real loose up there. He forced himself to think about not being too overanxious, and he took the first pitch just outside for a ball.

"Come on, ump, that hit the corner," shouted Mike Plank, pacing in the Pirate dugout.

Joey readied himself, and on the next pitch, he rifled a line shot just over Bruce Plank's head into left centerfield for a base hit, scoring Davey and Georgie.

"Way to go, Joey, way to be,"shrieked the normally laid back Billy, who had already finished his sideline throws.

The Mets bench and their group of supporters cheered loudly, and screamed for more as Billy, their star hitter, came up to the plate. Lou and everyone else knew an extra base hit would give the Mets an almost insurmount-able lead. But, on the other hand, should the Pirates retire Billy, it could cause a momentum-swinging situation, despite the Mets having just scored two runs. Billy was THAT good.

Lou, Billy, and everyone else would have to wait a little longer, as Mike Plank replaced Spurgen with Lenny Fielder. Fielder was the hardest thrower in the league, and if he could have his control, he stood a better chance of getting Billy out than Spurgen did, not to say that Billy was overmatched against any pitcher. He wielded a strong bat, period, and everyone at the ballpark knew it.

Billy steadied himself in the box, and prepared himself to do battle. The Pirates, both on and off the field, shouted encouraging words to Lenny Fielder.

Billy was first-ball swinging, and he lashed out at Fielder's high hard one, sending it to left center. Spurgen, now in the outfield, looked somewhat awk-ward going for the ball, but he indeed corralled it to retire the side.

As Billy went back to the bench for his glove, Joey was waiting for him and, in an attempt to interject a small amount of levity into a tense moment, said to Billy: "Don't worry, pitchers aren't supposed to hit."

Billy smiled, and said to himself what he really wanted to say out loud to Joey, which was: Am I really a pitcher? Am I doing the right thing?

Billy walked with a bit of uncertainty towards the mound. It surely felt strange for him to stop there, rather than continuing past both the mound and second base, and on into center field. He knew, as he began the first of his eight warm up tosses, that all eyes on the Pirate bench would be glued to him. A head coach will always tell his players to watch an incoming pitcher; check his deliv-ery, his follow-thru and most importantly, his speed. There would have been very little at this late stage for the Pirates to learn from watching a George Porter, Al Gustafson, a Joey Harrison, or even an Ike Eichorn warm up. All of these pitching mainstays were familiar to all the teams in the league. But here now was Billy Jeffries on the hill, someone none of them had seen at that position before, and of course, there couldn't have been a more pressure packed situation for Billy or any of them.

On the field, each infielder was, with curiosity, watching Billy warm up when they weren't taking grounders thrown by Ronald.

On the bench, Lou Skinner and Paul Dodsworth paced back and forth. Chris Conley, Donnie Bowman, and Eddie Howe were leaning against the dugout fence. Al Gustafson had already left the field with his parents, to be driven to the emergency room at the local hospital, where the ankle would be examined.

Of course, not only was an inexperienced Billy on the mound, but Lou also had to do some other shifting in the field to account for the absence of both Billy and Al. So, as Vinnie threw down the last of Billy's warm-up throws to Joey, the Mets showed a defense of Ronald at first base, Nicky at second, and Joey at short, but Marc Davidson at third, with Ike in center field now, flanked by Davey Filstein in left, and Scotty Edwards in right.

"Okay Billy, let's throw strikes," shouted Lou, as Lenny Fielder stepped in to lead off. Mike Plank had instructed Fielder to take a strike, hoping that Billy's inexperience on the mound would lead to control difficulty.

Billy gave himself a brief pep talk, and with a "here goes" attitude, went into his wind-up and threw a strike, causing excitement on the field and in the Mets' dugout.

"Way to start off," Vinnie said as he threw back to Billy. Fielder took Billy's next pitch low for a ball, and the following pitch was in the same location. The count was 2-1, but Lou was still encouraged, because Billy was around the plate.

The next pitch was a good one, but Fielder hit it hard. Fortunately for the Mets, it was a one-hopper back to the box, which Billy fielded and calmly tossed over to Ronald for the first out.

Man, that felt good, Billy said to himself, as he got ready to face Freddy Pointer. Pointer had a habit of leaning close to the plate, and this undoubtedly unnerved Billy, who walked him on five pitches.

With a two run lead, Lou shouted out to his fielders that the batter was the important out.

"Make sure of at least one, infielders," he yelled, which meant that if a ground ball was hit, they should be careful, taking their time to throw accurately to second base for the force out, or perhaps making the surer out at first. To the outfielders, the situation was that on a base hit, they could let the lead runner go to third, for it was of paramount importance that the batter not get to second, into scoring position.

Billy, somehow sensing that the batter, Don Hearn, would be taking a strike here, let up a tad on the first pitch. Hearn indeed let it go by, and it was called a strike by the home plate umpire. The next pitch was a beauty on the outside corner, and Hearn dribbled it down to first, where Ronald, remembering Lou's words, picked it up, declined a throw to second, and ran to first base for an unassisted out. Two outs now, and there was a controlled frenzy on the part of the Mets' dugout and their supporters.

The excitement quickly subsided, however, as Pirate lead off batter Eric Stein, anticipating the same softer first pitch from Billy, guessed correctly and lined it into center field for a base hit. The ball was hit hard enough, so that Pointer stopped at third once his coach saw that Ike had fielded it cleanly.

Lou called time and went to the mound, and ushered Vinnie, Joey, and Nicky over to discuss what to do if Stein attempted to steal second. They unanimously agreed to have Vinnie try to gun him down, again dismissing Lenny

Fielder's importance at third in this case. Before leaving the mound, Lou reminded Billy he should not anticipate that any of the Pirates will be taking a strike here, so he had to come in with some heat right away.

Billy looked in at Vinnie's target, and uncorked a high, hard one that John Simon could not get out of the way of, and the ball struck Simon on the batting helmet. Simon went down to the ground instantly, as time was called.

Billy looked on in disbelief, and in an instant he had realized his greatest nightmare. Why, oh why, thought Billy, did I volunteer to pitch?

At that moment, however, John Simon arose from the turf, dusted himself off, and upon informing Mike Plank that he was okay, trotted down to first, to the sound of applause and cheers on the part of all spectators as Eric Stein advanced to second base.

Despite this huge relief, Billy was in tears, with his back to home plate, feeling ashamed of himself for crying, yet fearful of continuing.

In a rush, Melvin Jeffries, sizing up the situation, ran down from the bleachers and over to Lou, and quickly related to Lou what Billy had said at home last night.

"He's afraid of how badly he can hurt someone, coach," Mr. Jeffries offered.

"I understand," replied Lou. "Thanks for letting me know, Mel."

Lou again called time, and walked out to the mound. As Vinnie and Joey also approached, Lou motioned them away. Billy still had his back to home plate, and so he had no way of knowing that his father had just spoken to Lou. He was, therefore, shocked to hear what Lou had to say, as he felt his coach's arm go around his shoulders.

"Billy, the batter's okay. That's what they have helmets for. I know, you probably want to come out of the game right now, but I can't let you. I don't care if we lose this game. If I take you out now, I know you'll never pitch again, and I can't have you go through life being afraid of that. Believe me, Billy, I'm doing this because I care about you, not because I want you to be forever tormented. You know I've always been honest with you guys, and that's not about to change now. Think about it this way. What if you were the batter, and someone like Lenny Fielder hit you with a pitch. It would take an awful lot to get you out of the game, wouldn't it? Well, getting hit with a pitch does hurt, but it's not that serious. Do you see John Simon crying over there? No, he wants to score the winning run. I hope he doesn't, but if he does, it'll be with you on the mound, and no one else. You're a great player and a great kid. You're thirteen years old. Do the same things bother you now that did when you were nine? Let the Pirates beat us for the right reasons, not because of something that happened a long time ago."

A smile came to Billy's face. "My Dad's been talking to you, right, coach?"

"Yes, Billy, and I only wish you had talked it out with him sooner. He loves you, and he would have told you how to handle it."

"Better late than never, coach," Billy replied, as he wiped his eyes with his sleeve, turned around, and faced home plate. "I'm ready to do it."

"Atta boy, Billy, and remember......."

"I know," said Billy, "nothing but heat."

"You got it, pitcher," shouted Lou as he trotted back to the dugout, pausing to look up towards the stands where he gave a thumbs-up sign to Melvin Jeffries.

"Force at any base," screamed Dodsy from the bench, as Vic Spurgen came up to the plate, bases loaded and two outs.

Regaining his composure, each pitch Billy threw now seemed harder than the previous one, and with a 2 and 1 count, Spurgen weakly grounded it in the hole between short and third. Joey, playing deeper than normal, made a fine stab to come up with the ball on his back-hand, but he wisely held onto it, as he really didn't have a play anywhere, with his feet planted on the edge of the outfield grass. With all baserunners advancing, the score thus stood at 6-5 Mets, and who was up for the Pirates but none other than the great Bruce Plank.

Billy knew he had to block everything out of his mind but the batter, and certainly a formidable batter it was.

Both benches were shouting encouragement to their star players. Billy knew, from watching Plank at bat dozens of times while patrolling centerfield for the Mets, that anything shoulder high to Plank would be flirting with disaster. Vinnie was aware of it too, and he'd give Billy a low target.

Even Plank sensed the gravity of this pressure-filled situation and although confident, he wasn't his usual boisterous self now, as he knocked the dirt from his spikes with the bat, straightened his helmet, and proceeded to dig into the batter's box.

Joey shouted over to Billy, to offer some encouragement.

"You can do it; let's go, Billy," yelled Joey. The entire infield picked up on Joey's lead, and their voice levels seemed to be in competition with those of the three runners - Stein, Simon, and Spurgen. If they had thought about it, all of the fielders and runners would have realized that they were not only trying to encourage their side, but to relieve the anxiety they each felt inside as well.

Lou yelled over to Ronald that on a would-be base hit to the outfield, to run over to the appropriate area to help line up the throw, and he reminded Billy to back up home plate. Lou also yelled out to Ronald to block any low throws to first from the infielders.

Clearly, you could feel the tension and excitement in the air, as Billy looked at Vinnie's target and prepared to pitch to Bruce Plank.

The first pitch was a bullet on the outside corner, just above the knees, not in Plank's wheelhouse, and he took it for a called strike one.

"That's one! Come on, Billy," screamed Dodsy, who was trying to remember if he had a good luck position at which to stand now.

The next pitch was at the letters, but a little inside, for ball one, evening the count at 1 and 1.

Billy's next service was low, and Vinnie had to get down on both knees to block it. The count was now 2 and 1.

Billy settled himself and uncorked a beauty of a pitch, near the outside corner of the plate, but the umpire felt it was off the mark, and called it Ball Three. That really put the pressure on Billy, who had to come in with a strike, but needed to serve it with heat, for an aggressive hitter like Plank would probably not be taking here. The pitch came and Plank, swinging all the way, lined it over third, but foul by about two feet.

This was now the moment of truth for both sides, as the count was full. Billy wound up and fired, and it was a bit inside, and possibly would have been Ball Four, except that Plank was taking no chances, and swung at it, popping it foul into short left field. Joey, running at an angle and at full speed, nearly duplicated his sensational catch from earlier in the game, but he just couldn't reach it, despite diving for it. So, the count remained at 3 and 2.

Plank steadied himself in the box, while Billy pounded the ball into his glove, made sure he had the grip he wanted, and went into his motion. With everything Billy could muster, he let it go. The pitch was probably not where Billy had wanted it to go, for it was shoulder high and appeared headed for the heart of the plate, and Plank swung hard. But he swung too late, and the only contact the ball made was with Vinnie's glove. Strike three, end of game, end of season.

Everyone seemed stunned for a moment: Billy, who'd made the pitch of his life, Bruce Plank, who couldn't believe he'd missed it, and every player, coach, and spectator there, who'd probably never seen this superb hitter strike out swinging like that before.

It then became a mob scene near the mound, as the Mets players came from all directions to get to Billy, to shake his hand, to rub his head, and to hug him.

Dodsy didn't know which went higher in the air, the scorecard he'd flung skyward, or his own body as he was jumping up and down.

Lou, of course, was in the middle of the hugging scene, trying to congratulate each of his players one by one, but found it impossible, so he ran over to the stands and embraced Lisa and his kids.

"I don't know how you got him to continue, coach, but it sure worked. Great job," offered a congratulatory Melvin Jeffries.

"It was all Billy's doing. That's a fine boy you have there, Mel."

"We never had our doubts about him, coach, but I think he did until today," Claire Jeffries added.

"Well, the important thing is that he made the effort. Had he lost, it would have hurt for awhile, but after the dust would have settled, he'd have known he'd tried, and that's the important thing," replied Lou.

"Lou, honey, I think you're needed down there. It looks like they're beginning the award ceremony," said Lisa.

"Okay, well, I'll see you all later," beamed a happy Lou Skinner as he trotted back down to the dugout area.

Chapter 39

The award ceremony promised to be a lengthy one, starting with the presentation to the second half regular season division winners, the Reds, who were all on hand, and would be introduced by their manager, Pete Billigan.

After the Reds received their trophies, the Pirates were next, and it would be a double presentation - one for their first half conquest, and the other for being championship series runners up. The Pirates were obviously upset to have lost the series, but two trophies apiece would, no doubt, soften the blow. Mike Plank called out each player's name, congratulating every one of them for a job well done. At the end of his speech, he also mentioned the great playing of both the Reds and the Mets, reminding everyone that any of these three teams could have been champs this year. Not one person there could argue with that. In closing, Mike Plank stated, "I'm proud to be a part of a league as well-run and as competitive as this one is, and that's what it's all about."

League President Jake Collins stepped back up to the mound area and bellowed, "Now, a team that did it the hard way, finishing in second place during both halves of the regular season to the two fine teams you've already heard from, and winning both the semi-finals and the finals in dramatic fashion, here are the Mets, led by their head coach, Mr. Lou Skinner. Lou?"

Lou ambled over towards the mound, to the applause of everyone there.

"Thank you, Jake. First, I'd like to congratulate the Reds and the Pirates on fine seasons and playoffs. You both made my heart beat a lot faster these last few weeks. I'd also like to thank all the families of my players for their support and understanding, and that includes my wife Lisa, and our kids Peter and Amy, who put up with me and understand that my life's passions are the three of them, plus baseball, although not necessarily in that order. Hey, that's just a joke, honey. Now, I'd like to introduce my team. First, our manager and statistician, and a person who's as much a part of this team as anyone, Paul Dodsworth. Paul will have the entire season's stats ready in about five minutes, right Dodsy?"

"Not quite," Dodsy answered shyly, nevertheless feeling extremely proud at this moment.

"Next," Lou continued, "a player who is equally adept in the infield and the outfield, and who really has improved, Marc Davidson."

"Now, a great kid with a superb glove, who's on the verge of becoming a good hitter too, Davey Filstein."

"A player who always hustles, and who got a big hit for us today, Chris Conley."

"Here's a guy who I believe nearly doubled his batting average this year, testimony to his fine work ethic, Eddie Howe."

"Next, is one of the fastest learners we have, and a real pleasure to coach, Donnie Bowman."

"Now, our leadoff hitter, a guy who started a lot of rallies for us at the plate, and killed a lot of opponents' rallies in the field, Nicky Plugman."

"Here is a fine athlete. Without a doubt, he's the fastest runner in the league, and he's saved many runs in the field with his speed and his excellent glove. The Walk Man, Ronald Carson."

"Better change that to the Running Man, coach," yelled out Dodsy.

"You're right, Dodsy. Next, folks, is a hard nosed player who comes from a great family of athletes, and I only hope that he channels his energy in the right direction, Scotty Edwards."

"Now, for a player who's not here, and I hope he's okay……."

"Wait a minute, coach, here I come," shouted Al Gustafson, as he got out of his father's car and slowly hobbled towards the field. It had only been a bad sprain; nothing broken.

"Well, then, let me start over," a relieved Lou Skinner responded. "Here's to one half of a great one-two punch on the mound, although after what I saw in the bottom of the sixth today, that may have to be amended to become a one-two-three punch, the modern day matinee idol, Al Gustafson. Al, in case you don't know it, we won," laughed Lou as he shook Al's hand.

"Don't worry, Al," yelled out Scotty's brother Jason. "I've got it all on video tape."

"Including my fall at first base?" Al countered.

"Yep, I got a real good angle on that. You can come over and watch it anytime."

"Thanks, Jason," Al replied.

Lou started again. "Here's a kid who's as mature and level-headed as anyone I've ever seen. No matter how pressure-packed the situation, he's always calm, yet focused on the mound. A great pitcher, Georgie Porter."

"A slugger supreme who drove in a lot of big runs for us this year. A great player - Ike Eichorn."

"A real favorite of mine. He's always got something to say, but he also talks big on the field with his performance. A born leader, Vinnie Panzini."

"Did you say born eater, coach?" said Chris Conley.

Vinnie walked over to Chris and feigned a mean demeanor as he got real close to him, but then gave the high five sign, which Chris returned to him.

Lou continued. "Now here's a kid who I can only say this about. Every parent should have a boy like him. He's just a joy to be around, well liked by everyone. He had a great game today and he'll have many more in the future. Here's Joey Harrison."

"Finally, here's a young man whose exploits on the field are mind-boggling, yet it was his courage to do something today because of a very special friendship he has, and because he's a team player in every sense of the word, that will forever stand out in my mind - Billy Jeffries."

"Ladies and gentlemen, boys and girls, let's hear it for this year's champions, the Mets," Jake Collins shouted, and the applause was considerable.

As the Mets went to collect their gear, grudgingly posing for pictures taken by their families, and commencing to talk about a team dinner (pizza at Lou's house), Bruce Plank walked over to their dugout.

"Hey, Panzini, good game. I don't know if the best team won, but I'd have to say you guys are good."

"Thanks, Brucie. Just for that, I won't tell you how beautiful my trophy looks," Vinnie answered.

"Hey, Jeffries, you're a pretty good pitcher. How come we didn't see you pitch before today?"

"Well, er, you see," started Billy, before Joey moved in to take over the conversation.

"Billy was our secret weapon, that's all. We were saving him," said Joey.

After Plank left, Joey turned to Billy and said, "I'll say you were a secret weapon. Such a secret, his own team didn't know."

Billy smiled, put him arm around Joey, and said, "Don't feel bad, Joey. It was a secret to me too."

"Say, Billy, now that you're a star pitcher, what are you going to do for an encore?" questioned Dan Harrison as he approached the dugout to pick up Joey.

Billy smiled once more and replied: "I'm gonna work with Joey more on his pitching. I tell you, it's a lot easier in center field."

With that, Billy and Joey left the field together, two great players, two great friends.

THE END

Acknowledgements

I am blessed to have family members who are not only equally passionate about sports, but who gave me splendid advice and direction.

To my son, Scott - As you can see from the wonderful lyrics he wrote for the foreword, he has such an incredible gift. We share a lot together, a bond over the years that was at least partially framed by the love of baseball. I'm sure he won't mind my relating that it was with tremendous anticipation that my wife Joy and I signed him up for instructional baseball when he was 5. The first day, he is out in the outfield, and I notice him picking daisies off the grass, or as I like to refer to it, my "oh well, shrugging my shoulders moment", as I assumed we would have to move on to something else for him/me to enjoy. However, in a complete reversal of fortune, he gets up to the plate and slugs a long shot over the left fielder's head, running the bases to turn it into a home run. That was the start of a wonderful period in our lives, now that he was hooked, and he went on to play Little League, competing at a high level, as well as cheering me on in my softball league days. This book in large part captures the mutual enthusiasm he and I have shared over the years for baseball.

To my brother Tommy - I harken back to the days when as teenagers, we played an entire 162 game schedule of Strat-O-Matic Baseball (probably in a month's time). To this day we do admit to "adjusting" Mantle's card, so had we kept individual stats The Mick might have batted .900 in our league. We had several talks about this book I wrote, and not only did he give me encouragement, he offered some key assistance in several areas, and I credit the book's title to him. My brother reminds me every day that the Peter Pan in both of us is what keeps us going.

To my son in law Sam - I utilized his keen eye to offer needed advice and constructive criticism on certain aspects of the book. I was torn among three possible timelines - the 60's when I was a kid, the 80's when my son played, and the current time line. Ultimately, I ruled out the current era, since baseball has taken a back seat to other sports, and I also omitted the 60's and settled on the 1980 decade, and it was he who counselled me to make sure the period the story took place was congruent with what was going on in the world at that time. He created a zip file for me so I could take my printed manuscript (I had actually first written this book several years ago, but never published it), type it into this file, and edit it. I am grateful for his guidance.

Now, a shout-out to my wife Joy. She has always understood my fervor for sports, and baseball in particular. Though the women in my family are far from being sports addicts (my daughter Traci, who at age 11 pulled off an unassisted double play by tagging out a runner at between first and second and then racing home to tag out a would-be runner at the plate, stopped playing when she broke a fingernail), they have understood the importance of sports to me. Joy always encouraged me to play sports, even when my time was taxed by playing in two softball leagues at the same time. She'll glance here and there at the TV screen when the Yankees are on (perking up when Aaron Judge is at the plate), but that is the extent of it. Thank you Joy, for having allowed me to enjoy my passion over the years.

Lastly, I have incredible memories of playing ball over 50 years ago, as well as coaching, and I would like to share this with my friends in the Arverne Schoolyard. To The Clovers out there and the other teams I was on or coached, or competed against, I cannot think of a better place and time to have grown up (or did we?).

Les Koenig Bio

LES KOENIG has spent close to 50 years in the Housewares industry and while he has traveled extensively all over the world in search of, and to develop household products such as tea kettles and marble kitchenware, baseball is his first love and writing this book is his "baby". A graduate of Queens College in New York, Les wrote a weekly satirical sports article called "The Games People Play" for the Long Island Graphic newspaper.

He currently resides in Florida with his wife Joy, and is fortunate to have both of his children Traci and Scott and their families near by.

This is his first novel.